KAT BALL

Southern Girls

First published by Ink & Honey Press 2025

First edition

ISBN (paperback): 979-8-9936791-1-2
ISBN (hardcover): 979-8-9936791-0-5

This book was professionally typeset on Reedsy.
Find out more at reedsy.com

This book is dedicated to the memory of my mother — a true Country Girl — and for my grandmothers, and every mother before them, whose love and strength still light the way.

Contents

Author's Note

Hey y'all!

I wrote this book like a series, each chapter with its own opening and closing song.

If you want to set the mood, play the first 30 seconds before you start a chapter, and the closing song when you finish, like rolling the credits after a scene.

It's totally optional, but if you want the full experience, I've put together an official playlist on YouTube:

Southern Girls: The Soundtrack
  YouTube.com/@KatBallMadeIt

1

The Girl with the Bag

♪ *Southern Girl* - Maze feat. Frankie Beverly

The sun sliced through the blinds like honey as the ceiling fan clacked overhead. The steady pulse of the house reminded Marie exactly where she was, back in her childhood room, wrapped in wood-paneled walls.

Spring semester had wrung her out, so being back in her own queen-sized bed for the summer, with it's soft mattress and familiar weight, let her bones finally exhale.

She tried not to think about the bed she'd woken up in the morning before she came home, but her body remembered.

Her phone buzzed on the nightstand, the screen lighting up: 8:47 a.m., May 2016. She didn't have to check to know who it was.

JAQ: You up?

She was awake. Had been awake.

She lay there, suspended between rest and the hum of something she couldn't yet name, her lilac scarf pressing her pixie cut flat, like petals pressed between the pages of a book.

The phone buzzed two more times in her hand.

JAQ: *Come over tonight*

JAQ: *I missed you*

Marie texted back.

Relax! I'll be there before dinner.

She set the phone down and peeled herself out of bed, padding barefoot into the hallway, drawn by her favorite scent, onions in oil.

That smell meant something was already in the skillet, something seasoned.

Music floated from the kitchen as Marie leaned in the doorway like her body hadn't caught up with her yet.

"What you cooking?" she yawned.

Her mother didn't turn, still working the skillet. "You said you wanted to do our cleaning routine a day early, but I see you ain't say nothing about helping with breakfast."

Marie grinned at the tease. "Food tastes better when you cook it."

She glanced around, then asked, "Where's Daddy?"

"In the garage," her mother said, shaking her head. "Been out there all morning trying to fix that mower."

Marie laughed, picturing him hunched over the stubborn machine.

When the eggs were perfectly firm and cheesy, the potatoes tender yet crisp, and the toast golden, they sang between bites and sipped orange juice at the sunlit kitchen table.

When the plates were scraped clean, her mother turned up the Funkadelic's "(Not Just) Knee Deep" and passed Marie the lemon polish and a fresh cloth.

They danced through the house the way they always had. Mama tackled bathrooms and glass. Marie hit furniture and floors, noticing how the rooms seemed smaller than when she was a kid.

Oil soap, bleach, and glass cleaner tangled in the air like a family recipe, and by the time it settled, the house gleamed like it was ready to testify.

Her mother stepped back, satisfied. "I'm claiming the rest of my Friday."

"What you got planned?" Marie asked, tossing the last rag into the laundry pile.

Her mom smirked. "Probably hit a thrift store... or two."

Marie shook her head, laughing. "Don't go too crazy."

Back in her room, she lit her mango candle, showered long and hot, then wrapped herself in her favorite fuzzy robe before pulling her Louis Vuitton Keepall duffle out of the closet.
Jaq's mother had gifted it to her last Christmas. "Something told me you'd be traveling far one day," Mrs. Bell had said, her eyes soft with pride. She remembered the golden hardware catching the glow of the tree.

The buzz of her phone cut through the memory.

JAQ: Bring the wok. Been feening for your rice

MARIE: Bet. Been feening for it myself

"Okay…" she murmured looking through her closet. "I need sleepover-comfy and just-in-case-we-go-out. Do I need heels? No. But also… maybe."

She rose on her tiptoes to snag her block heels from the top shelf. She needed enough options to feel polished without looking pressed.

Today called for a cream ribbed tank, wide-leg denim, and her gold vintage clip-ons. Simple yet sparkly.

Her mother peeked in just as she zipped her bag.

"You gonna be back for church on Sunday?"

Marie smiled. "Yeah, I'll meet you there."

In her mind she had already decided that this would be the last year she'd allow herself to be paraded around and introduced to her mother's church friends and their painfully eligible sons.

She kissed her mother's cheek, waved through the garage to her father, and climbed into her black Tahoe, the one he'd brought at the auction and cleaned so good she could catch her reflection in the hood.

She remembered being twelve, asking her father why he didn't have to go to church. His answer had been simple: "We are the church."

The sun pressed hot against the windshield, sweat already gathering behind her knees.

She tried the radio before the AUX cord.

"It's your boy Bobby J at WBLK 98.7 Vibe of the South. This one is for all the ladies who still smell like cocoa butter."

The music hit for "Sweet Thing" by Rufus featuring Chaka Khan. Marie grinned, turning it up. Her hands tapped the steering wheel, light and sure, like she was in the studio herself.

By the time she turned into the gated community where Jaq lived, she'd dropped the volume low, still humming.

She checked her hair in the mirror. Edges still laid, name plate necklace still bright on her collarbone.

She reminded herself to use Jaqueline's full name around Mrs. Bell, who swore the "Jaq" was too boyish and harsh for her daughter.

The Bell home rose ahead of her, all glass, and stone. It was the kind of house that looked like it should come with a brochure. And the art inside, was real art, with names she actually studied in class.

Mr. & Mrs. Bell had done it by the book. Degrees, matching Benzes, two kids.

They were always flying or on call when their children were younger, but made it up in square footage and gifts, even if those gifts got opened over speakerphone.

For Marie, it wasn't just about the house, it was Jaq. She missed her, the sleepovers, and the sisterhood.

She rang the bell, wok under one arm, duffle on her shoulder.

Mrs. Bell opened moments later with a grin and a mimosa, silk press flawless.

"It's so good to see you," she crooned, hugging Marie's neck.

"You didn't have these hips spring break," she teased, making Marie spin. "What are they feeding y'all at Spelman?"

Marie laughed. The Bell women were loud, possessive, and never missed a detail.

She met Jaq in seventh grade. She was the quiet new girl in the stiff uniform, Jaq was the opposite and pulled her in and kept her since day one.

"Bestie!" Jaq's voice echoed down the staircase.

Her hair swung like choreography, and a gold anklet winked against her sepia skin with every step down the stairs. Barefoot, draped in a silky matching lounge set, she swept into the room—hugging Marie with one arm, snatching the wok with the other.

"I missed you and all, but I'm also starving." She said playfully. "I wasn't playing when I said I've been feening."

Over the years, preparing meals for the Bells became Marie's way of showing gratitude, for the space and the softness. Before long, she always had their kitchen smelling like the back door of a restaurant.

Jaqueline helped sometimes. She was cracking eggs directly into a pan like she was on Food Network when the front door beeped.

"Must be Bryson," Jaq said, grabbing the sesame oil from the cabinet and setting it down by the La Cornue Château range.

Marie dumped the rice into the wok just as he entered the kitchen, broad-shouldered like he paid taxes there.

He acknowledged his sister first. "What's up?"

Then he turned to Marie. "How are you here before me, and I live here?"

Marie didn't look up from the wok. "I know that's not how your mama taught you to greet company."

Jaq rolled her eyes, already annoyed. "Y'all, please don't start."

Bryson grinned, raiding the fridge. "I'm just saying. You here so much, we should've invited you to the family reunion."

Marie scoffed. "Forget the reunion. Y'all should put me on payroll."

Bryson chuckled grabbing a bottle of water. "Maybe if you learned how to cook something other than chicken fried rice."

Marie huffed. "Says the person who ate four bowls last time."

"I do what I can to support the arts," Bryson said, grinning and reaching for the rice with a fork.

Marie swatted at him with the spatula, catching the glint of the vintage Cartier watch on his wrist, the one his father passed down to him back when he turned sixteen. He backed off, hands raised in surrender.

Later, bowls full, they all gathered at the dinner table beneath a chandelier that probably cost more than Marie's Tahoe.

Mrs. Bell gave her that soft-smile-hard-question combo.

"What are you taking next semester?"

Marie straightened. "Advanced studio, Color and Composition II, and a seminar on Black abstraction."

Mrs. Bell smiled and tilted her head, like she was intrigued.

"And you, baby?" she asked, turning to Bryson.

He shrugged. "Consumer Behavior, Digital Marketing Analytics, Advanced Public Speaking…"

Mrs. Bell smiled bigger. "Advanced Public Speaking? I like that you're challenging yourself."

"How about you, Jaqueline?" Mr. Bell finally asked from the head of the table, deep voice laced in expectation.

"You know its never too late to…"

"Still running my business," Jaq interrupted. "Sales are up."

Her father sighed. "We gave you every opportunity to not have to hustle like we did."

Jaqueline shrugged. "I'm not hustling. I'm building."

"In the guest room," her mother added bluntly.

Jaq lifted her chin. "Not like I'm up there playing. I've got spreadsheets, inventory…cash is flowing."

Mrs. Bell's brow arched, but she held her tongue.

"Building a beauty empire in the same room where y'all used to argue over Chris Brown. I think it's impressive." Bryson said, trying to ease the tension.

Mr. Bell softened. "We just want more for you. That's not a punishment."

No one disagreed, but no one answered either.

After dinner, Marie and Jaqueline retreated upstairs for silk robes and face masks.

"Girl! Let me show you Tariq," Jaq said, flashing her phone. Tariq was tall, clean-cut, and fine in the way that knew it. "I met him at that networking event I was telling you about."

Marie smiled. "He's cute."

"And smart," Jaq grinned. "He said I have a strong product, just need to make the story just as strong. People will stay loyal to the brand when they connect with the woman behind it."

"One thing," Marie said, grinning. "Your mama will have a *cow* if you bring him around with all that gold in his mouth."
She laughed, already picturing the look on Mrs. Bell's face. She doubted if Jaq's parents, or even her own, had any real understanding of gold teeth—the art, the history, the statement.

Marie remembered reading that dental modifications using gold and precious stones dated back to ancient civilizations, like the Mayans and Egyptians, marking status and power. The Bells would've had a full set, for sure.

By eleven, the house was quiet.

At one, Marie's alarm vibrated against her pillow.

She was awake. Had been awake.

She got up and slipped into her Air Max Plus, muttering a half-hearted, "Forgive me, Lord," for going sockless.

Every shadow felt like a witness, every creak a warning as she slowly made her way down the hall and descended the staircase. She paused at the patio door, pulse hammering, then slipped into the hot thick night air toward the pool house.

She put her right thumb on the door's security pad.

Green. Click.

Knowing the layout by heart, she headed into the cold dark towards the fridge.

Leaning back against the island, she took a long steady sip from a bottle of water.

She felt Bryson settle beside her, still warm from his bed. He didn't speak, just watched her.

When she finally paused, he took the bottle and set it down on the marble. He closed the space between them until he was standing directly in front of her, his gaze locked on hers, then he leaned in, close enough for his breath to brush hers.

The kiss came hungry but controlled, his hands slowly sliding under her silk robe, fingertips stopping at the bare curve of her hips.

"We skipping layers now?" he murmured, smirk brushing her mouth.

She didn't answer, just smiled, as her hands found the back of his neck.

♪ *After the Dance* - Marvin Gaye

2

The Girl Who Stayed

♪ *Cleva–* Erykah Badu

Saturday morning was quiet. Too quiet. Like the walls had been up all night watching her sleep, waiting for her to decide something she kept putting off.

Jaqueline lay in bed for a moment. The sheets were cool and heavy and the mattress was firm, just the way she liked.

Her vision board was tucked beside her desk across the room, half-covered in pink sticky notes. There was a photo of a spa storefront with "Buttah Haus" written across the top in sparkly pink ink. The name was loud, but the idea still lived in her chest like a secret too fragile to release into the air.

A Spelman flier peeked out from behind a printout of her very first online sale. It was a little creased, but still proof she could do this, for real.

It was her room, her house, and her life, but lately it all felt a little too... preserved. Like she was an artifact her parents didn't know what to do with.

She peeked across the hall into the guest bedroom although she knew her friend wasn't there. Marie liked to wake up at the crack of dawn to meditate and exercise and...all power to Marie.

She found her right where she knew she would be, in the basement gym.

"Alright," she said smacking 'End Run' on the dash of the elliptical.

"It's going on Brunch o'clock and we've got places to be."

Marie hopped off the machine and pulled out her earbuds.

"I forgot how aggressive you are in the morning." She said, catching her breath. "Oh, and just a heads up, I'm leaving early tomorrow morning to..."

" ... go to church with your mama." Jaq finished. "That's exactly why today is for the soft life. To the shower you go."

By nine they were dressed and smelling like Flowerbomb.

By ten, their feet were soaking in bowls of jasmine-scented water at Diamond Nails.

Erykah Badu's "Bag Lady" floated through the speakers and a soft breeze from a discreet fan kissed their edges.

Jaqueline's phone buzzed with an order confirmation. She ignored it, leaning back while the technician worked her magic.

Beside her, Marie was deep into her phone, thumbs moving fast like she was trying to hide something in plain sight.

"You know you can relax now, right?" Jaqueline said. "Who do you keep texting anyway?"

Marie looked up. "I was just checking something."

Jaqueline clocked the way she blushed and tucked her phone under her thigh.

After manicures and pedicures, they had brunch at The Gardenia Room. They ordered way too much. Shrimp and grits with truffle oil, a tower of cinnamon-crusted French toast, and biscuits so flaky they crumbled. It almost felt like old times.

Marie's phone lit up again and she flipped it over.

Jaqueline pretended not to notice. She just sipped her sparkling water as the sun poured in from the restaurant's sunroof.

Marie finally put her phone back down on the table. "I miss this," she said, soft and honest.

"Yeah," Jaq smiled. "Me too."

"Soooooo…" Jaq said, trying to keep the conversation going. "Is that your little 'boo' in Atlanta you keep texting? "

Marie cleared her throat and laughed "Girl, no. You know I've been all about my books and my art."

"Who says you cant have books, art, and a bae?" Jaq said shrugging her shoulders.

She hinted toward a table with a group of handsome young men who seemed to be about their age. "We might be able to find you somebody cute in here." She said, almost in a whisper.

Her eyes grew wide. "Then we could double date." Jaq was getting too excited about the possibility.

"I promise you'll get your double date one day." Marie assured her. "But I *need* to be focusing on making a little money this summer. Good art supplies are *not* cheap."

Jaqueline sucked her teeth "I feel you, but you are way too strict on yourself. I just want you to have it all."

"Awwww!" Marie fake cried. "I want it all for you too, friend."

They both laughed as they did their version of the scene from The Color Purple movie where the sisters are playing patty-cake in a field of flowers. Jaqueline spotted movement at the next table. She gave him a scan. Navy Polo tee. Clean white Forces. Perfect teeth. Sharp fade. His eyes kept darting to Marie like they had a secret.

"Three o'clock," Jaqueline said, voice smooth.

Marie didn't even blink. Just sipped like she hadn't heard.

16

Jaq leaned in. "You know exactly who I'm talking about."

"So what, you want me to blow him a kiss?"

Jaqueline grinned. "I want you to live a little."

Marie rolled her eyes. "You talk to him."

"Please, he's already decided. I'm just the sidekick."

Marie finally caved and turned, just a glance. Jaqueline caught the pause, the brief hitch in her friend's smirk. She knew he was fine. He knew he was fine. Not in an annoying way, just that I-drink-my-water-and-mind-my-business confidence that always worked on girls like Marie.

"The man is trying to play it cool." Jaqueline said

Marie smiled into her glass.

They pretended not to watch as the guys stood up to leave. Jaq swore Navy Tee did a stretch just to flex. The friend beside him nudged his arm. Something passed between them, then he turned and started walking their way.

Jaqueline sat up straighter and whispered, "He's coming. Don't embarrass me."

"Don't embarrass yourself," Marie muttered.

He stopped right at their table, flashing a smile.

17

"Hey," he said, eyes on Marie. "Not to interrupt, but your laugh, it made my whole day."

Jaqueline could've collapsed on cue. Polite? And direct? What in the rom-com?

"I'm Dre," he said, extending a hand.

Marie shook it, but didn't blink. Jaq knew her well enough to catch the tiny delay before she spoke. "Flattered, but I'm spoken for...and he's kind of territorial."

Jaqueline bit the inside of her cheek to keep from cursing. The lies. Why was her friend like this?

"I'll let y'all get back to it," he said, backing off with a nod. "Just had to shoot my shot."

After the guys left, Jaqueline turned, brows raised high.

Marie rolled her eyes. "You need a hobby."

"I have one. It's you and your tragic love life."

Back at the Bell's, Jaq asked if Marie wanted to help pack up some orders. She'd lent a hand a few times before and it usually involved music and the two of them dancing and laughing as they worked.

"Girl, yes!" Marie smiled. "You know I look forward to being paid in Shea butter, right?"

Jars lined the shelves of her workroom, each one topped with a matte gold lid and labeled in soft pink. The air carried traces of lavender and bergamot, like the room itself was exhaling calm.

Jaqueline had the grades, the acceptance letters, even a scholarship. But instead, she stayed, took her savings and flipped it into something uniquely hers.

She was making money. She wasn't broke. She was still in her childhood bedroom, but just for now.

After they worked and danced up an appetite, Marie pulled together what the Bells had in their kitchen and turned it into a rich, garlicky Alfredo with broccolini and garlic knots.

Jaqueline walked in and paused just as she was plating everything. "Okay Chef!"

Mrs. Bell came in behind her and headed to sit down at the table. "Mr. Bell and Bryson had a tee time this evening. Something about getting in nine holes before sunset."

"I've always wanted to try golf," Marie said, finally taking a seat.

"You know," Mrs. Bell said, skipping right past her comment, "One of the girls from our neighborhood goes to Spelman too. You remember Vanessa, don't you?" she asked, looking directly at Marie.

Marie nodded her head, wiping her fingers delicately on her napkin. " Yeah, I remember Vanessa from some of Jaqueline's birthday parties."

Jaq thought back to those parties. Vanessa always had a way of shifting the vibe, usually by loud-talking about whatever extravagant birthday her parents were plotting next.

"She's majoring in Psychology." Mrs. Bell added.

"Oh," Marie said reaching for another garlic knot.

"Today we hit that flea market." Jaq inserted, changing the subject. "The one we used to go to when I was little. Can you believe all we got was an old rusted picture frame?" She laughed.

"Wait till I flip it." Marie said pointing her fork in Jaqueline's direction. "You'll see."

Mrs. Bell smiled, and for once, didn't ask any follow-ups. "To girls with vision," she said, lifting her water glass with that signature tight smile.

Jaqueline clinked hers in return. "Vision, taste, and a little chaos."

Marie pointed her fork at her. "Don't forget delusion."

"Necessary," Jaqueline said, eyes wide. "You seen the dating pool?"

Mrs. Bell raised a brow but said nothing.

Marie laughed softly. "You'd think you were out here struggling."

"I am struggling," Jaqueline said. "A young man with taste. And perhaps a passport. The bar is not low, it's buried."

Her mother's eyes twitched upward at the corners, like she might've actually found it funny, but wasn't about to admit it.

"I just want someone with basic home training," Jaqueline continued. "Like… can he vacuum and iron a shirt? That's it. That's the application."

"'Home training is generational," her mother said dryly. "You don't fix that with cologne."

"Cologne's a strong motivator." Marie said, grinning.

Her mother actually chuckled at that, low and under her breath. A rare sound.

Jaqueline caught it and paused, startled by how good it felt to see her laugh, really laugh, not just nod politely like she was playing hostess to her own daughter.

Marie leaned back in her chair and stretched. "Maybe the next one will surprise you."

Jaqueline raised her glass again. "To a future husband with throw pillows and emotional range."

Marie raised her glass. "And steak in the fridge."

Mrs. Bell raised hers last. "Lord help us all."

That night, after she hugged Marie and bid her goodnight, Jaqueline lay in bed unable to sleep, half-scrolling, half-letting her thoughts wander to things she didn't usually make space for.

Her phone buzzed.

TARIQ: You up?

She blinked at the screen. A small smile tugged at the corner of her mouth.

JAQ: For now.

TARIQ: I was thinking about you earlier. Wanted to say hey before the night got away from me.

JAQ: Hey.

Seconds later, the phone rang.

She hesitated, then tapped accept and lay back into the pillows.

"Hey," she said again, this time out loud.

His voice was low but clear. "Hey."

There was a pause, then he added, "I've been thinking about you."

She smiled, but kept it hidden in her voice. "Is that right?"

He chuckled. "You're… different than I expected," he said.

"Different how?"

"You're sharp. But you've got a softness too. Most people hide that."

Jaqueline felt herself blush and was glad he couldn't see her face. "Maybe I just forgot to tuck it in."

"Well, I noticed," he said. "And I liked it."

She let out a quiet breath, the warmth of his voice spreading across the phone line like a blanket.

"You surprised me too," she said. "I thought you were gonna be more…"

"Rough around the edges?"

"A little."

He laughed. "Give it time."

They both laughed at that.

He cleared his throat. "I don't know if this is forward, but… I'd really like to see you again. Properly. Somewhere with less noise."

She turned onto her side, her voice quieter now. "I'd like that."

There was a pause, then a soft hum of approval from his end. "Good. That's all I needed."

Neither of them made a move to hang up.

Eventually, she whispered, "Sleep well, Tariq."

"You too, Jaqueline." He said before ending the call.

She lay still for a moment, phone resting on her chest, the edges of a smile still tugging at her mouth. Then the floor creaked somewhere in the house. It was normal, familiar, the kind of sound homes make when they settle.

But moments later, she heard movement from the back yard.

She sat up a little, phone still in her hand.

Maybe her brother was home and had come into the main house for something. The pool house had always been Bryson's unofficial bachelor pad.

Sometimes he'd pop into the main house for toilet paper, food, or anything else he didn't feel like driving at least 30 minutes to get, depending on what you were willing to settle for.
And sometimes, he had company.

Back in his senior year in high school, there was Sierra. Pretty, athletic, went to school in the town over.

She left behind a fake eyelash and a nearly empty bottle of curl smoothie.

"Let's see who it is," she muttered to herself, already halfway out her bedroom door.

Jaqueline crossed the hall to the guest room, eager for a clear view of the backyard. When she stepped inside, the room was dark and empty.

Marie's phone glowed softly on the nightstand, screen unlocked like it had been abandoned mid-thought.

Jaqueline hesitated, but her eyes dragged toward the light anyway.

A message thread.

B: You left this. Figured you might need it tonight.

She blinked, pulse quickening.

Underneath the text was a photo. A lilac headscarf draped across a dresser she knew too well. It was Bryson's dresser, in the pool house.

Her throat tightened as she shut off the screen, shutting out the glow, shutting out the proof, but the image was already burned into her.

♪ *Didn't Cha Know* – Erykah Badu

3

The Girl Across the Street

♪ *Cranes in the Sky* - Solange

Vanessa opened the curtain with two fingers.

Across the street— no, across the cul-de-sac, as her mother insisted on saying, the black Tahoe had just pulled into the Bell's driveway.

She wasn't spying. She was assessing. There was a difference. Spying made you desperate.

She moved back toward her vanity, lit by a soft glow. Her room was all cream and blush tones, minimal but intentional. A gold-framed quote that read 'Elegance is refusal - Coco Chanel' sat on the vanity next to a Diptyque candle she never lit.

From downstairs, her mother called:

"Vanessa! Could you come help me with these napkins!"

She rolled her eyes, checked her reflection, then headed downstairs.

In the formal dining room, her mother was folding linen napkins, probably for some event at the country club. The same club where Mr. Bell had been "so helpful" with the board placement.

Vanessa sauntered in and asked. "Do you think Mrs. Bell and I have an understanding?"

Her mom didn't look up immediately, just pinched the next napkin into a triangle before folding.

"An understanding?" she asked, her tone so neutral it might've been legal testimony.

Vanessa nodded slow. "Like… she knows I'm the one she always wanted for Bryson."

At that, her mom gave a small laugh, the dry kind she used when she wanted to buy time.

"Vanessa. Baby. Mrs. Bell wants what's best for her son."

"I *am* what's best," she said.

Her mother looked up. "You were the plan, sure. But people don't always stick to the plan."

"She's known me since we were kids. She picked me for the cotillion."

Her mother didn't answer. She just gave her that same look she gave

27

servers who forgot the lemon for her tea— cool, polite, and full of silent judgment.

Vanessa went back upstairs.

She laid across her bed, pulled out her phone and began typing:

VANESSA: Hi Mrs. Bell! Realized we have your serving dish. I can drop it off now...

She stared at it for a second, then deleted the whole thing.

She opened her images instead. Buried in her Favorites folder, was a photo from prom.

Her, grinning wide in her high-slit gown, and Bryson, standing next to her in his tux, half-smirking.

She'd grown up hearing his music through open windows, pretending not to notice when he'd gotten taller, stronger.

That night, when he showed up on her porch with a fresh haircut and crisp boutonnière, her heart had fluttered like it meant something.

They'd taken pictures while his mother fussed over every pose. Bryson had stood still, polite, patient.

The dance itself had been a blur of colored lights and songs that didn't quite land. They didn't dance much. He checked his phone a lot, but when one of her favorite songs came on, he joined her on the floor, just long enough for her to think maybe the night was turning around.

Afterward, they grabbed drive-thru milkshakes and sat in his car for a bit, windows cracked, radio low. The air was thick with that almost-summer warmth. He'd thanked her for coming, said he was glad his mom made him go.

It wasn't romantic, not really, but she held onto it anyway. The look, the song, the weight of his hand on her back in the photo.

She went to his page. It was still public. Of course it was. Bryson Bell didn't have anything to hide, or at least, he pretended not to.

The most recent post was a blurry pic of a field at sunrise with no caption.

She kept scrolling. Bryson and Jaqueline in matching tees at a family reunion.

And then…

A photo of a hand holding a sketchpad. Not his hand. Not his sketchpad.

At first glance, the drawing on it looked simple: A gold necklace.

But the devil was in the details. The chain twisted just slightly at the top, like it had been tugged mid-movement. On the skin behind the it, just barely visible, were tiny sweat droplets.

It was intimate. Not just a sketch, a piece of memory.

Bryson's caption was "She's cold."

He didn't say who, but Vanessa knew. It was that girl. The one with the black Tahoe.

She saw them together her freshman year. They were on the shaded path by the art building. He was smiling, but not the smile he used at parties, this one had softness.

She pretended not to see them and not to feel the burning in her chest, the heaviness of something old and cold unthawing.

That same semester, her roommates wanted to hit a soul food place for 'Girls Night'.

Vanessa almost didn't go, but the group begged, and she liked being begged.

The hostess led them through the packed dining room, all exposed brick and reclaimed wood.

They were halfway to their table when she saw them again, tucked into a quiet two-top by the window.

Bryson was laughing, real laughing, like teeth showing, head back laugh.

Marie reached across the table and touched his hand. Bryson didn't move away, he leaned in closer.

The leash tugged.

"C'mon Matisse," Vanessa mumbled.

She hadn't planned to go out this early, especially on a Saturday, and especially not looking like this. She was wearing a hoodie from the homecoming she didn't even stay for and yoga pants that used to hug tighter.

Matisse needed to go, and Vanessa figured she could sneak a block without being seen.

Right as she reached the edge of the driveway, there she was, Mrs. Bell, with one hand on a copper watering can and the other already mid-wave.

"Vanessa!" Her voice rang.

Vanessa smiled, quick and tight. "Hey, Mrs. Bell."

"Out walking the pup?" she asked, glancing down at Matisse like he was a dust mop.

"He gets antsy if I don't take him out early."

Mrs. Bell nodded. "That's good. Routine is important. Keeps things... steady."

There was a pause. The kind that felt like it had subtext braided into it.

"I was just telling your mom the other day, our families used to seem so close."

Vanessa swallowed, throat suddenly dry.

"Yeah, we've known each other a long time."

Mrs. Bell tilted her head, watering the base of a rosebush now. "History has a way of coming back around, especially when the roots are deep."

Vanessa nodded slowly. "True."

And then Mrs. Bell flashed her perfect, practiced smile.

"I won't hold you. See you around."

Vanessa kept walking, then turned the corner, giving Matisse's leash a gentle tug as he stopped to sniff a bush.

She let him lead the way, until they got to the final mailbox on the block. Just as she reached into her hoodie pocket her phone buzzed.

It was her dorm-mate Amani, who was home in Texas for the summer but still all up in Vanessa's business.

AMANI: Hey roomie! You never told me what happened with Khalil that night

VANESSA: Nothing. It wasn't him. It was me.

AMANI: Ha! Translation: He wasn't Bryson.

VANESSA: You're annoying

VANESSA: And right

AMANI: Wild! You got Cash and Khalil practically auditioning to be your man.

VANESSA: Bryson's different

AMANI: Sis. He is tall, fine, and emotionally unavailable in a fitted tee.

VANESSA: I'm serious. He's the package.

AMANI: Package? Ma'am.

VANESSA: Shut up

By the time she rounded the corner back onto her street, the air still held that early-morning quiet.

She paused at the foot of her front steps, letting Matisse tug at the leash and nose around the flowerbed.

She opened her texts and scrolled to Bryson's name.

She could already hear Amani roasting her from states away, so she locked the screen before she could make a mistake.

She glanced across the street to where she'd seen Mrs. Bell earlier.

It hadn't been what she said, it was how she said it.

"History has a way of coming back around, especially when the roots are deep."

Vanessa had smiled, played it cool, but she'd been thinking about that line. It sounded like an invitation wrapped in warning.

She stepped inside the house, letting the door ease shut behind her with a soft click. She dropped her keys into the ceramic bowl by the door and stood still for a moment, like she was waiting on a sign, or maybe just the silence to say something back.

Maybe she didn't need to send a text. Maybe she just needed to keep playing it smart.

Maybe Mrs. Bell would help her find the right way in.

Vanessa exhaled, then turned to head upstairs. She showered and got dressed in a pleated white tennis skirt and soft yellow tank. With her sunglasses on, fresh lip gloss, and keys in hand, she felt ready to tackle the world, or at least matcha.

The bell above the coffee shop door chimed, and cool air wrapped around her as she stepped inside. It was a welcome contrast to the late-morning heat still clinging to her skin.

Vanessa scanned the space without being obvious about it. Same soft jazz hum underneath the hiss of the espresso machine. Same regulars hunched over laptops like the world depended on their work.

And then she saw him.

He was near the window, tucked behind a chipped wooden table, head down, flipping through a worn paperback.

Vanessa didn't change pace, didn't straighten her posture or tilt her chin. She ordered her drink like it was just another Saturday and eased into her favorite corner seat two tables away, just close enough to watch without making a scene.

Her matcha arrived, layered and bright. She stirred it slowly, letting the green swirl into the almond milk.

Then, casually, she crossed her legs. The hem of her skirt slid up just enough to show the toned line of her thigh. She took a long sip, watching him over the rim of her cup.

He looked up from his book once, but it was enough.

Vanessa waited a beat, then stood and walked toward the napkin stand next to his table like she was just grabbing a straw. The oldest trick in the book.

"Matcha, huh?" she said casually, turning just enough so her gold hoops caught the light.

He looked up with a slow smile. "Trying to stay healthy. Doesn't mean it tastes good."

"Sacrifice," Vanessa said with mock solidarity. "A man who suffers for the greater good."

He laughed, closed the book partway. She clocked the title, *The Fire Next Time*. Predictable in a fine-and-socially-aware kind of way.

"You from around here?" he asked, already leaning back in that easy, interested way some men have when they think they're about to be lucky.

"Born and raised," she said. "But I left for school."

"Let me guess....an HBCU?

Vanessa raised an eyebrow, impressed despite herself. "How'd you know?"

"You've got that posture. Smart, but a little dangerous."

She smiled, slow and deliberate. "That's cute."

They traded small talk. His name was Anthony, he was a marketing major, and he lived in one of those overly renovated lofts with bad parking and a rooftop grill nobody used.

"You know," he said after a few minutes, "there's a vinyl night at that spot down the street. You should come. I'll be there with a few friends."

She tilted her head, thoughtfully. "Maybe."

"You got a number I can text?"

She paused just long enough to make him think he'd won something. Timing was everything, give too fast and you're easy, wait too long and you're cold. She'd perfected the middle ground.

She handed him her phone and he tapped something in. She didn't check it before tossing it back in her purse.

She let the silence stretch a little.

"You're cute, Anthony."

She walked back to her seat and didn't look back again. When she finished her drink, she pulled out her phone, and blocked Anthony's number.

♪ *The Great Pretender* - The Platters

4

The Girl Who Knew Better

♪ *Prototype* - Outkast

It started as nothing. It had to. If she admitted it started as something, on purpose, then she'd have to own what came after.

Jaqueline was still on the phone with her new boyfriend so Marie slipped out of the room, giving them space to trade sweet nothings and lie about their curfews like 16-year-olds did.

She wandered downstairs into the living room, not really looking for anything, just bored.

On the ivory sectional, one of Bryson's game controllers blinked. 2K was paused on the screen.

She smirked and reached down, not because she wanted to play, but because she could. She'd overheard Mrs. Bell sending Bryson off to the farmers market.

He'd been gifted a black-on-black BMW 535i for his 17th birthday, and now he treated every errand like a victory lap.

She resumed the game, handling the controller like she knew what she was doing. She didn't. Just wanted to win the quarter before heading back upstairs.

She must have gotten a little more invested in the game than she intended, because she didn't even hear him come back in.

"You're trash." Bryson chuckled.

Marie didn't look up. "I don't really do sports games. I play Black Ops."

Why did she *always* feel the need to explain herself?

She didn't say anything else. She had the Heat and Hawks neck-in-neck and needed to concentrate.

He sat down next to her, not too close, but close enough for her to smell the outdoors on him.

"Me too. Whats your gamer tag?" He asked.

"PowerpuffPlaya" she said, instantly regretting not coming up with a quick petty comeback.

He laughed. "I knew you were a nerd, but damn!"

She should've said her gamer tag was "DeezNutz." Why hadn't she thought of that sooner?

That next Saturday night, Marie was tucked in her room, deep into a solo run on Black Ops when Bryson's username popped up in her messages.

BryHardOrDie: Jump in and run some. We're short one.

She rolled her eyes and typed back:

Tapping out. Church in the AM

She didn't know if this counted as using God's name in vain, but hopefully it was a good enough excuse for him to let her off the hook.

She was nervous. About the mission. About accidentally doing something stupid and having some random boy from Chicago or Atlanta laugh her off the server.

BryHardOrDie: Cool pray 4 better game

PowerpuffPlaya: Ur gamer tag is BryHardOrDie

BryHardOrDie: What? It goes hard.

PowerpuffPlaya: Boy stop! It goes lame.

It didn't take long for the messaging to leave the console.

He'd passed his number smooth one Saturday night after dinner.

"You forgot something."

When she looked down, his number was on a folded napkin.

"In case you ever wanna settle the rematch score." He said with a smirk.

She saved him as "B," just so it wouldn't look like much of anything.

At first, their texts were just about the game.

Then it turned into things like how they both could tell when Jaq was about to lie... or cry.

When Bryson went off to Atlanta to attend college, the messages started coming in about nothing.

Remind my sister to watch her gas tank.

Or just,

You straight?

She never knew how to respond to any of these "nothing" texts. Most times she responded with a meme. The dumber the better.

She told herself it was just Bryson being Bryson— friendly, familiar. But every time his name lit up her phone, her pulse jumped before she could catch it.

The dynamic changed again when Marie packed her bags for Atlanta that next fall. For years, she'd pictured it being her and Jaq walking those campus greens together. Instead, she and Bryson ended up being neighbors, with Spelman and Morehouse split only by a single road.

One Friday evening she got a text from him that said:

You go to Market Friday or you too fancy?

Marie blinked at her phone checking the time. It was late enough that the booths were winding down and the DJ was probably packing up.

She stared at the message for a second, closed her messages app, then reopened the thread and typed...

Not too fancy just can't be spending money every week.

She sent it before she could overthink it. It was too real for a meme. He replied in under a minute.

Say less. What dorms you in?

Marie blinked again. She sent the name of the dorm, then typed:

You can't come in tho they're strict AF.

He responded:

Meet me outside in 20?

She stared at that one for a while, long enough that her roommate, Jordyn, finally looked up from her laptop.

"Are you okay?" Jordyn asked.

Marie still stared at her phone.

Jordyn swiveled in her desk chair like she'd been waiting for this exact moment to pounce.

"You've been staring at your screen for five minutes." Jordyn said. "Who's that?"

"It's... someone I know from home. He asked if I wanted to meet up."

Jordyn perked up immediately, abandoning whatever spreadsheet she had open. "Wait..."

Marie gave her a look.

"Are you gonna go?"

Marie hesitated. "I don't know. It's already late, and I haven't even started my..."

"You've been here two weeks," Jordyn interrupted, already standing up. "That's way too many days of going to class and eating dining hall food. You owe yourself. How much time do we have?"

Marie glanced at her phone again. "He said meet him outside in 20."

Jordyn clapped once, dramatically. "Perfect."

Marie didn't protest as Jordyn pulled open the closet door.

"I'm not saying you have to fall in love," Jordyn said, "But you do need to get out of this room before I file a wellness check."

She stood in front of Marie's half-closet like it had personally disappointed her.

"Okay, we're not doing a full thirst trap, but we're also not dressing like you're about to go to bible study."

They agreed on a white cropped tank and a light-washed pair of distressed high-waisted skinny jeans, cuffed neatly at the ankle.

Jordyn tossed her a lightweight zip-up. "You'll probably take this off in ten minutes but bring it anyway. The night might try to be nippy."

Marie looked at herself in the mirror, her pixie neat and slick, not a strand out of place. Her pulse, on the other hand, didn't get the memo.

"Text me if you need an excuse to leave. I can fake a family emergency so fast." Jordyn grinned.

By the time Marie made it out to the front entrance, the sun had dipped low.

Bryson was standing there in a Morehouse sweatshirt, sleeves pushed up to reveal his muscular forearms.

He held a brown paper bag out to her.

"Lemon pepper, extra wet. A fry might be missing."

Marie fought her smile.

"Strawberry, right?" He asked, handing her a milkshake.
He smiled slow and small, like the memory had been sitting right there, waiting.

They sat down on the edge of the plaza. Somebody was bumping 2 Chainz from a speaker in the distance.

Bryson stirred the last of his milkshake with his straw, not looking at her just yet.

"You been good?" he asked, voice easy.

Marie stretched her legs out, trying so hard to be casual. "Yeah. I've been straight."

He nodded like he didn't fully buy it. "Alright. Just make sure you stay that way."

She glanced over, eyebrow raised. "What's that supposed to mean?"

"It means, watch out for these dudes. Brand new Spelman girl with cute hair and a smart mouth? They're gonna be all in your face."

Marie smirked. "I can handle myself."

"Oh, I know," he said. "I'm just saying, if somebody get too comfortable, starts tryna run game," He paused, then added with a lazy grin, "Text me. I'll pull up."

She sipped her milkshake to buy time, then said, "I've been focused on school. On my art."

He didn't say anything, but she could feel him listening.

"I never really had time to be..." She paused, eyes fixed on the condensation sliding down her cup.

Marie didn't explain. She didn't say that no guy had ever really gotten past the outer layers.

He didn't push. Just nodded slowly "That's cool. That's smart."

"What about you?" she asked.

He gave a quiet laugh and shook his head. "Nah. Nobody serious. I've been chilling."

Another beat passed.

"Good to know," she said, and didn't explain what she meant.

More silence.

"I missed you," he said finally.

Marie took a slow sip of the milkshake. "Yeah. Me too."

It wasn't dramatic, no declarations or social media reveals, but Marie and Bryson just started showing up for each other after that.

They didn't come to events together, but they always ended up next to each other. Bryson had a way of slipping into the seat beside her like it was already saved. She'd roll her eyes, but she never told him to move.

They never made it a thing, but people noticed. The way she leaned into him when he spoke. The way he watched her like the everything else was background noise. The way they always left, not quite together, but not exactly apart. If anyone asked what they were, she just said, "Oh, it's not like that."

When Jaq came for homecoming, Marie and Bryson had to chill. No inside jokes. They kept it light and friendly, but Marie felt every inch of the distance. All weekend, she thought about telling Jaq. At brunch. At the step show. Even in the middle of a grocery store run when the three of them were joking in the snack aisle. She thought maybe Bryson would say something first, drop a hint, offer a look, but he never did. And she didn't either.

Before they could make sense of any of it, it was Christmas break.

Marie's parents had been threatening to take a holiday cruise for years, and this year, her father found a deal he couldn't ignore.

Her mother had texted once. She didn't say 'No parties. No boys.' Marie would *never*. She just said "Don't forget to water my peace lily by the sink."

A knock at the door came just as she was finishing her hot chocolate. She didn't jump because she already knew who it was.

Bryson stepped inside holding a slim black box, velvet ribbon tied too perfectly to be from the mall.

"Merry Christmas Eve!" he said handing it to her as he walked in. "Don't go crazy. It's not much."

Marie closed the door behind him and untied the bow slowly, like whatever was inside might vanish if she moved too fast. Inside was a gleaming gold necklace.

14 karats, no diamonds, no extras. It was just her name, scripted in soft curves, anchored to a fine chain that caught the light when she turned it. The weight of it settled into her palm.

"Bryson..." she started.

"I know you don't like flashy," he said quickly. "But I figured... you know, its simple."

"Simple." Marie repeated with an eye roll.

"Want me to put it on?" he asked.

She hesitated, then turned her back to him. His fingers were warm and a little shaky.

The chain sat elegantly just above her collarbone.

"Your sister's gonna ask." Marie said, turning back to face him.

The smile on her face was real, but so was the worry behind it.

Bryson didn't even blink.

"Just tell her it's from someone who knows you deserve nice things."

She half-laughed, trying to shake off the warmth rising in her chest.

The air inside felt too charged, so she suggested they go out back, down the sloped hill and past the trees where the neighbors couldn't see.

"You sure you wanna do this?" Bryson asked, his voice low, teasing. "I'm not tryna corrupt nobody's daughter."

Marie rolled her eyes. "Boy."

He grinned. "Aight then. Watch and learn."

He lit the pre-roll like he'd done it a thousand times, and took the first hit easy, like his lungs knew the shape of the smoke.

He looked good out here. Unbothered.

When he passed it to her, her fingers brushed his. She tried not to make a thing out of it. She was already trying not to make a thing out of everything.

Marie held it like he showed her. Inhaled too quickly and coughed hard.

Bryson laughed but didn't say anything. Just handed her his water bottle.

She waved him off and took another drag, but slower this time.

"You're a natural," he said, watching her.

Marie smirked. "Liar."

They passed it back and forth, and the cold didn't matter as much anymore.

She couldn't remember what they'd been talking about before, but everything slowed.

He moved closer without touching her. She didn't move away.

"You good?" he asked, voice low but steady.

"Yeah," she answered.

The air between them buzzed like static.

"Can I kiss you?" he asked.

"Yeah," she breathed, then closed the space between them before the word had even settled in the air.

The kiss was warm and slow, a little clumsy at first, the kind of clumsy that happens when two people want something badly but don't know if they should.

Marie felt it in pieces: the press of his lips, the way his hand settled on her waist. Her chest barely brushed his, but the contact sent a low, blooming heat through her ribs. She felt it in the curve of her spine, in the flutter behind her knees.

She let herself fall into the softness of it and when her fingers brushed against his chest, she felt his heartbeat quicken.

When the kiss finally broke, she didn't open her eyes right away.

He brushed his thumb against her chin, then exhaled.

"I should go," he murmured.

"Yeah," she said, even though she wished he wouldn't.

She hadn't meant to get used to his place. But by the second week of the Spring semester, she was kicking off her shoes at Bryson's apartment like it was her own.

It was small, but he had made it his. He had a soft leather couch, an old record player to spin, and always kept a cashmere candle burning.

He told her he'd paid for it himself with some crypto play he got in on early, held his ground when everybody else bailed. "You gotta be patient," he said. Marie knew that tone. He could've been talking about her.

His parents didn't know about the apartment, not really. It wasn't the most airtight setup, but Bryson had a way of making things work that had no business working.

Marie didn't ask too many questions. She just liked being in on it. It felt like something grown. Like being invited into a part of his life no one else got to see, his real life.

One Sunday, Marie found herself back at his apartment. She hadn't meant to stay long, was just supposed to drop off his flash drive, but ended up on his couch, helping him fold laundry while they listened to records.

He looked at her, really looked, long enough for her to notice, and for the moment to stretch thin. "Are we gonna talk about the kiss?"

Marie froze. "The kiss?"

He laughed once, short and low. "Yeah, the kiss."

Her eyes dropped to the floor. "It was... a moment."

"Yeah, it definitely was." He said.

She exhaled through a smile she didn't mean to let out. "What do you want me to say?"

He shrugged. "That you felt something. That I'm not crazy."

Marie tilted her head, heartbeat climbing. "You're not crazy."

His fingers brushed her cheek, then lingered at her jaw. Her breath caught when his lips met hers, soft at first, before deepening into something more sure.

Her fingers hovered at the hem of his shirt, then finally slid under the fabric.

His hands found her like they'd been waiting, her skin burning in places he barely touched.

Everything felt deliberate, like each touch carried a conversation neither of them had been brave enough to have out loud.

When he paused, both of them breathing heavy and quiet, she felt something settle deep in her chest, the feeling when you know nothing's going back to how it was.

Neither of them said a word, he just took her hand and, without hurry, led her down the short hallway.

Everything that followed was careful, intentional, like a promise neither had planned to make.

When the room fell back into focus, she lingered, fingers sketching thoughts she didn't say onto his chest.

"You good?" he asked, lips brushing the top of her head.

"I'm good." Marie whispered.

He smiled and pulled her closer, one arm draped around her back like he meant to keep her there forever.

And maybe, for a little while, she believed he could.

♪ *Promise*- Ciara

5

The Girl Who Carried Grace

♪ *I Know I've Been Changed* - LaShun Pace

Renae had always loved Sundays. They reminded her of hot combs hissing and gospel humming from the radio in her grandmother's kitchen.

She stood in the mirror longer than usual that morning, dabbing her under-eye with concealer, smoothing the dress she'd worn only twice before. Not too flashy, but not plain either. She wanted to look nice for church, but if she was being honest, for her daughter too.

Marie said she would meet her there and Renae had smiled, of course. A mother didn't show hurt in the face of an "I love you," even when it came tied to a goodbye.

She didn't blame her. The Bell house was beautiful, Jaqueline was her best friend, and they had always welcomed Marie like family.

But there were months when it felt like Marie spent more Saturday mornings laughing in their kitchen than her own. When Marie was younger, Renae told herself it was all harmless, sleepovers and privilege and different kinds of comfort.

But now, nearly grown, Marie still disappeared into that world, leaving Renae at home folding laundry.

She wasn't bitter, it was something quieter, lonelier.

She pressed her lips together in the mirror. A smile smoothed over the ache.

As a little girl, Renae never cared much for climbing trees or jumping fences. While her siblings and cousins played tag, she sat behind their clapboard house, beneath the dogwood trees with her dolls.

She didn't just play with dolls. She played mama, always mama, holding them close like a dream she could already feel coming true.

Most of her dolls were secondhand. The plastic on their faces had started to fade by the time they were hers, but she didn't mind. She treated every one like it might breathe if she prayed hard enough.

Renae and her husband had tried, year after year. Four pregnancies. Four losses.

By the second miscarriage, she stopped putting her hands on her stomach when she prayed.

By the third, she stopped looking at baby sections in stores.

By the forth, she'd given her last doll, her favorite one with the curls, to a neighbor's daughter without saying goodbye.

Then, Marie came.

She came after the nursery had already been packed away. After they had stopped talking about it.

Over time, the ache dulled into something quieter, manageable. Now, it lived mostly in the silence between moments and in Sunday mornings.

Renae drove with the windows down to let in the morning air. It was warm and earthy with whispers of cut grass and distant smoke. The road wound past weathered barns, crooked rows of mailboxes, and open fields where cotton used to grow wild and proud.

There was something sacred about Sunday mornings in the South, before the heat settled in, before the world got loud. Out here, it felt like time moved slower, and her thoughts could breathe.

She smiled to herself as the church steeple rose into view, white against the blue sky.

She loved her church. It had stained-glass windows, a professional choir, and the feeling of real congregation.

Renae parked and sat in the same section they always claimed. Third row from the back, not quite under the air vent that blew cold enough to make you bring a sweater in July.

She heard her heels before she saw her and turned just enough to catch a glimpse.

Marie wore a cream dress, cotton-silk blend, with a soft square neckline and short sleeves. It was modest enough for church, but still hugging her hips. Her perfume drifted faintly of vanilla and citrus, mixing with the smell of old hymnals and polished wood.

A tan blazer was neatly draped in the crook of her arm. She remembered the vent.

She's growing up, Renae thought, but she's still mine.

Marie caught her mother's eyes and smiled. She slid into the pew with a whispered "Hey, Mama," and a soft touch to Renae's arm.

"You made it," she whispered resting her hand gently on her daughter's knee.

Marie grinned. "Told you I would."

Renae nodded, eyes facing forward. The choir had just started in on *I Need Thee.*

For a second, watching her daughter from the corner of her eye, she wished Marie had come home Saturday night instead of Sunday morning.

She wished she'd been there for dinner, and folded her legs up under her on the couch the way she used to, or helped Renae re-twist her locs while some old Western played.

She wished she hadn't missed the smell of grits and eggs that morning, hadn't arrived smelling like someone else's house.

There was a time Marie would rest her head in Renae's lap and ask her questions about God and boys and what she might look like on a magazine cover someday.

But girls grow. They pull away like tides, polite and unintentional, so she didn't hold it against her, but she held it.

The pastor's voice cut through like warm light.

"Beloved, we sometimes live with heavy hearts, burdens unseen by the world. You carry expectations, you carry grief, you carry the weight of what could've been or what will be. But God does not call us to carry these alone."

Renae's grip tightened around Marie's hand. She felt the press of years, the waiting, and the fear that her daughter, might also grow accustomed to carrying burdens in silence.

"There is blessing in open hands. Open hands that release control. Open hearts that admit they cannot always hold it together."

He paused.

"If you feel your hands clenching—over your past, your pain, your perfection—release it. Trust the One who carries more than you can ever bear."

Soft tears gathered behind Renae's eyes. She felt Marie shift next to her in subtle comfort, shared gravity.

Some weight had been shared in the pew, and the rest was theirs to carry in silence.

When they pulled back up to the house, Renae adjusted her hair in the car mirror before stepping out. She watched Marie quietly sling off her heels and step barefoot up the porch.

She didn't say anything yet. Just unlocked the door and walked them both inside. The scent of lemon and oil still lingered in the house from Friday's deep clean.

"Take that chicken out for me." Renae instructed. "I'm going to change clothes."

By the time she got back to the kitchen in her house dress and slippers, Marie was standing in the kitchen, still barefoot, staring out the window.

"You looked real pretty in that dress today," Renae said. "Had a little grown-woman shine to you."

Marie tilted her head. "What kind of shine?"

"The kind that makes people ask me questions after service." Renae answered, wiping at the spotless counter. "One lady asked if you was engaged."

She watched Marie bark out a laugh. "Engaged? To who? These church ladies stay trying to marry folks off."

"I said the same thing. But then I started thinking," she said carefully, watching her daughter. "You seeing anyone?"

"I don't know if 'seeing' is the right word," Marie mumbled.

Renae hummed. She wasn't surprised. She had come home once wearing a sweatshirt too many sizes too big, trying not to smile. Renae might not know all the details, but she could read her child better than anyone else.

"Then what *is* the word?" she asked softly.

Marie flinched like the question scraped something raw.

"It's complicated."

She let Marie sit with her own thoughts.

"He's good to me though," she finally said.

"Is he good *for* you?" Renae asked.

She didn't expect an answer right away. That pause told her everything she needed.

"I'll trust you to figure it out. But baby, don't wait 'til it hurts to be honest with yourself."

And with that, she let it rest. That was the deal with grown children, you couldn't really steer them, but you could make sure they had a compass.

She'd say a little prayer that evening instead. One of those mama-prayers. The kind you don't need to speak out loud because God already knows what's under your tongue.

Later that night, after the dishes were drying, Renae sat on the back porch. She could hear the cicadas humming, that humid song that let you know summer was sitting on your neck.

Her husband emerged from the house in his usual uniform of flannel pajama pants and a t-shirt and dropped down onto the metal chair beside her.

"Where's Marie?" he asked.

"Said she was gonna read, just wanted to be alone." Renae nodded motioning back toward the house.

"Lord, we got the moody one back under the roof again," he teased.

"Mm," Renae muttered, turning toward him slowly. "You remember that boy she used to hang around with? Jaqueline Bell's brother?"

Her husband blinked. "Tall one with the good posture? Always 'yes ma'am?'"

She gave him a sharp look. "Well, I'm starting to think it's serious."

"Serious like... I need to get the shotgun serious?"

She gave him another look.

He raised both eyebrows in surrender. "I ain't sayin' I'm against it. If he's the same boy I remember, he had some sense. Carried himself decent."

"She's doing good. Better than good. But you know how it goes, one misstep and it's all that work and potential out the window."

Her husband nodded slowly, picking at the seam of his pajama pants.

"She tell you what's goin' on?"

"Not directly," Renae said. "But I know. I can see it on her."

There was a pause, then he gave her a sly smile.

"Well, as long as she ain't askin' us for bail money or baby shoes, I think we can trust the girl to have some sense."

Renae narrowed her eyes.

He chuckled. "And don't forget, she's your daughter, not just mine. She got your spine."

"Mm. And your stubborn."

Her husband leaned over and kissed her cheek, then stood, stretching slow and dramatic.

"You stressin' yourself out," he muttered as he ambled toward the door. "Go say your little prayer and leave it with God."

"I already did."

"And?"

"And He told me to watch, not worry."

Just before bed, when the house was still and Marie was rinsing her glass in the kitchen Renae reached for the speaker on the counter and thumbed it on. A familiar hush of chords, Anita's voice, slid in like warm syrup.

Marie turned, brows raised, a smile threatening the corner of her mouth.

"You're not about to get sentimental on me, are you?" she asked, still holding the dishtowel.

Renae didn't answer. She just stepped forward and took the towel from her daughter's hand. She looped her arms around her and gave a small sway, slow and side to side.

"You used to stand on my feet and let me twirl you around to this," Renae whispered. "Now look at you."

Marie surprised her by resting her head briefly on Renae's shoulder, just for a second. Quiet, but enough.

They moved like that for a while, not quite dancing, not quite standing still.

♪ *Sweet Love* - Anita Baker

6

The Girl Who Made Plans

♪ *Don't Take It Personal* - Monica

The house was too clean. The air was too fake.

She hadn't said anything about what she saw on Marie's phone.

Not Saturday night. Not Sunday morning.

This wasn't some petty he said-she said beef. This was family. A wound made from inside the house.

Would she ask Bryson straight up, confront Marie, or go straight to Ma and let her handle it?

What if she accidentally set this whole house on fire by saying the wrong thing to the wrong person?

Just then, her screen lit up with a text.

BRYSON: *Got lavender scones from that bougie spot you like.*

Typical Bryson. Slipping in sweetness when no one was watching. Acting like they were all just one big, functioning family.

She shook her head and exhaled through her nose, amused and annoyed all at once.

She tapped her nails once against the back of her phone and slid it into her purse.

She walked past her bed, down the hall, down the steps, and out the door.

The drive was mostly muscle memory. Past the soccer fields where she and Bryson played exactly one season when they were young.

Past the corner store where Grandma used to take them for grape sodas, letting them pick out penny candy even when they'd been bad.

Jaq turned the wheel with one hand, the other draped across her lap. She kept thinking about all the times she caught Marie and Bryson mid-argument.
Not real, vicious ones, more like petty sparring. That time at a cookout when Marie called him "unseasoned," and he shot back something slick that made everyone laugh but made her squint.

Was that all cover?

How long had they been... them?

She exhaled sharply, tapping her fingers against the steering wheel. It didn't even feel like betrayal, not fully. It felt like some long, slow revelation, like watching a picture come into focus after standing too close for too long.

She made a right onto the winding, familiar street that led to Grandma Mayfield's. The houses here didn't change much, fresh paint jobs every few years, but the bones stayed the same, and so did the people.

Jaqueline eased into the gravel driveway and cut the engine. For a second, she didn't move. She stared out at the porch, where wind chimes swung gently in the breeze, then reached for her phone, almost out of habit, and scrolled to Marie's contact. Her thumb hovered over the name.

Not yet.

She tucked the phone in her purse, grabbed her keys, and stepped out of the car.

Whatever came next, it could wait until after sweet tea and a plate. Grandma didn't do family drama on an empty stomach.

The door was open, as usual, but she still knocked on the screen door and paused a moment before entering.

"Well look who the cat drug in," Grandma said. "Didn't know I needed to sweep the porch for royalty."

Jaqueline gave a small grin and leaned down to kiss her grandmother's cheek.

"I brought nothing but my mood," she said, dropping onto the sofa beside her.

"Mmm" Grandma hummed. "Well, I got peach cobbler and judgment. So we even."

Jaqueline exhaled hard through her nose, almost a laugh, but not quite.

The TV murmured soft in the background. It was always either old gospel videos or reruns of Bonanza, Grandma's other church.

She looked down at her lap and picked at the threads on her shorts.

"I found something out last night."

Grandma nodded like she'd already guessed. "Uh huh."

"I'm pretty sure Bryson and my friend Marie have been messing around behind my back."

Grandma sighed and folded her arms across her chest, a plate of cobbler resting on her lap.

"Well now," she said softly.

"What am I supposed to do about this?" Jaqueline asked.

Grandma reached over and laid her hand gently on Jaq's.

"You ever try to hold water in your hands?"

Jaqueline blinked.

"No matter how tight you cup 'em it still slips through the cracks." Grandma continued. "The truth is like that."

Jaqueline looked away at the television.

"I don't even know who to be mad at" she said.

Grandma reached over to the coffee table and straightened the coaster stack.

"They been walking a tightrope so long, they probably forgot what ground feels like," she said. "Don't mean they right. Just means they scared. Scared makes people reckless."

Jaq's voice dropped. "I just feel like a joke. Like I was the only one who didn't know what was really going on."

"That's the thing about secrets," Grandma said, turning to look at her. "They don't always mean people were trying to hurt you. Sometimes they were just trying to protect what little good they had."

Silence pressed in again.

"They should've said something," she whispered.

"You tellin' your mama?" Her grandmother asked.

Jaqueline shook her head. "No. I need to know more first"

Grandma raised one brow, slow and skeptical.

"Be careful with that need. You dig too deep, you might hit something you can't unearth."

"I just… I can't go back in that house yet. Not with him there pretending like nothing is happening."

Grandma nodded. "You don't have to. Hang with your grandma a little while." She said, headed to the kitchen with her empty plate.

Jaqueline leaned back, trying to slow her thoughts, when her phone buzzed.

A smile crept on her face.

TARIQ: What u doing this week?

JAQ: What's up?

TARIQ: Wanted to invite you to this rooftop thing

JAQ: What's the dress code? You got a plus one for my girl?

TARIQ: I might. She cute? What's her socials?

JAQ: She's not on social media. And all my friends are cute. Don't play.

TARIQ: She in witness protection or something?

JAQ: Lol possibly, but she's smart, sweet, single.

TARIQ: I have someone who might match her energy.

Jaqueline thought, maybe If Marie met someone new, this whole thing might just resolve itself.

Marie would get a new crush or finally confess. Either way, she would get some answers.

She wanted her to stop sneaking and start being honest. To own up to whatever had been happening under their noses. If Marie could say it, just once.

She didn't want to blow everything up. But one way or another, something had to give.

She stood, smoothing her shirt and reaching for her Sac De Jour just as Grandma Mayfield came back with two glasses of ginger ale, ice clinking as she walked.

"Thank you, Grandma," she said, "but I should be heading out. I've got a lot of orders to prep."

Her grandma raised an eyebrow, the way elders do when they don't believe a word you're saying, but love you too much to call you out in front of the Lord.

"You do that," she said.

The bell above the bookstore door gave a light jingle as she pushed her way in. She had no real reason to be here. Just needed somewhere quiet and she liked this place.

It was a little sanctuary tucked between a Jamaican spot and a boutique.

She wandered past the "Black Women in Literature" display and paused at a shelf with poetry.

"Jaqueline?"

She turned to see Vanessa standing across the aisle, looking like she'd floated in.

"Oh," Jaq said, forcing her smile "Hey."

Vanessa tilted her head. "You look cute. Are you meeting someone?"

"No"

Vanessa smiled like that answer was funny or sad. She couldn't tell and didn't care.

"Its actually funny running into you." Vanessa said "Your mother texted today and invited us to the brunch next Saturday."

Jaqueline blinked. "Us?"

Vanessa nodded. "Me. My parents." Her smile didn't budge. "You going?"

"I live there. So... yeah." Jaq said, picking up a random book.

There was a beat, the silence thick with polite warfare.

"Good," Vanessa said. "It'll be nice to catch up. All of us."

Vanessa's phone buzzed. She checked it, gave a polite smile, and said, "Gotta go. Hope you find something good."

"I always do," Jaqueline said.

As Vanessa headed down the aisle and out the door, Jaq let out a slow breath.

Seeing that no one was in her favorite chair, the comfy one all the way in the back corner, was enough to cheer her up, at least a little.

The side table was just the perfect height for using her laptop, but she wasn't exactly in the mood to work.

She pulled out her phone and messaged her mother:

Didn't know we were hosting a brunch.

It didn't take her long to text back.

MOM: I meant to tell you. Just something light for family only.

JAQUELINE: Vanessa told me.

MOM: Well yes, the Morgan's are coming. They are like family.

JAQUELINE: Wow.

MOM: What now?

JAQUELINE: You know how I feel about Vanessa.

They had to be seven or eight. They were playing Barbies in Vanessa's room, which was really more of a showroom than a bedroom. All pastels, monogrammed pillows, and custom shelving for the limited-edition collector dolls she wasn't even allowed to touch.

Jaqueline had brought her own Barbie from home, one with a twist-out and a hot pink trench.

They were setting up their "Barbie Boutique" when Vanessa paused mid-hair-brushing and said:

"You talk Black sometimes."

Then she tilted her head and added,

"Like the girls my mom tells me I'm not allowed to hang around."

Jaqueline had just blinked. She didn't say anything at first. Just gently pulled her Barbie back.

That night and asked her mama if she "talked Black." Her mother's silence was the first time she realized language could cut both ways.

JAQUELINE: I'll be there but don't expect me to smile about it.

MOM: *I never expect that from you baby.*

She leaned back in the chair resisting the urge to scream. Of course Vanessa knew about the brunch before she did.

She hated how her mom always tried to control everything, pulling strings like some puppet master in pearls. But then again, wasn't she doing the same? Steering Marie away from Bryson with this double date. They didn't even know she knew, yet here she was, plotting. The thought made her stomach turn, but not enough to stop her.

She opened her camera roll, scrolled to the picture she took of Marie looking fine in a soft blue dress, and hit send.

JAQ: *If your plus-one embarrasses me...*

TARIQ: *Say less.*

Jaqueline rolled her eyes but didn't fight the smirk tugging at the corner of her mouth.

She set her phone down, thumb tapping against her leg. Marie wouldn't like it if she knew she'd sent her picture, and honestly, Jaq was still deciding whether that was a betrayal or an act of service.

This was the only way to give Tariq's date a preview and maybe, just maybe, tip the scales in her favor.

Jaqueline exhaled, biting the inside of her cheek.

Outside, thunder murmured in the distance like someone whispering a warning.

She opened her thread with Marie and typed a message:

Double date with Tariq and his friend Friday night. I already told them we're pulling up. This is a YES thing. No excuses.

♪ *Got Friends* - GoldLink feat. Miguel

7

The Girl Who Showed Up

♪ *Boobie Miles* - Big KRIT

On Wednesday, they met up at park. Not the new one with the splash pad and tennis court, the old one, with faded basketball lines and rusty bleachers. The one where Bryson used to run summer drills and where Marie once sketched the same tree three different ways for her 9th-grade art project.

They shot around for a while, trading lazy shots and trash talk. Bryson let her win the first game then demanded a rematch. By the second, they were sneaking in playful bumps and low fives that lingered.

After the scrimmage they sat under the pavilion, drinking gas station lemonades and swatting at mosquitoes. Nobody else was around except an older guy walking laps.

Marie wore biker shorts and an over-sized shirt knotted at the waist. Bryson's eyes kept drifting, even when he pretended not to.

"So you just gonna act like you didn't cheat last game?" he asked, slouched low on the bench.

"I didn't cheat, I just distracted you and it worked like a charm."

He laughed, that real one that showed the dimple on his left cheek.

She sipped her drink and let the silence stretch a second too long.

Then she said it.

"So, I need to tell you something."

She ran a hand down her thigh, smoothing nothing in particular.

"Your sister's trying to set me up, like on a double date."

"With who?" Bryson asked.

"Some dude. A friend of her friend. It's Friday so I just, I thought I should tell you."

He squinted slightly, like the sunlight had shifted.

"You going?"

She didn't answer right away, just tucked a piece of hair behind her ear. Her voice came out more casual than she felt.

"I mean… " she said. "I told her I would."

She glanced over, but he was already looking away.

"But it's not like that," she added, immediately regretting it.

"I'm not trying to be messy. I just felt like you should know."

She waited.

"Nah. It's cool," he said, the words dry. "Look, you're single. We never said, you know, nothing official. So it's whatever."

She chewed her lip. That "whatever" tasted bitter.

Then he said, "He better pay."

He kept his gaze forward. "And open your doors. And keep his hands to himself."

She rolled her eyes but smiled, just a little. "Whatever."

A part of her wanted him to say something else. To do something else. To grab her and say he didn't want her to go, that it mattered. That she mattered. That this thing between them wasn't some lazy back-and-forth they had to keep hiding. She wanted him to tell the truth out loud, even if it messed everything up.

The silence between them had started to feel like a decision. Like they were both too proud or too scared to say what they actually wanted.

Then he stood up and walked to his car.

For a second, she thought he was leaving.

But now, here he was again, showing up in the way he knew how. Not with words, but with something he now held out like a peace offering.

Marie looked down at the green shoe box in his hands, then back up at him. "Bryson."

"What?" he said, too casual. "They're your size."

"That's not the point." She sighed, taking the box. "I told you to chill out with all this."

He shrugged, hands in his pockets. "They're just shoes." He said. "Plus you mentioned the art show."

"I barely mentioned the show." She said, opening the box.

It was a pair of gold Bottega Veneta Knot Sandals, delicate but structured, loud in the quietest way.

"You're gonna stand in front of your art, you might as well look like a masterpiece too."

She hated how her throat tightened.

"I can't wear these," she said, even though she already knew she would.

In her head, she'd decided if asked, they would be knock offs or something she found at a consignment shop. Jaqueline would roll her eyes but move on.

"You think money fixes everything, don't you?" Marie said quietly.

For once, Bryson looked like he wanted to argue, but couldn't find the words. He rubbed the back of his neck. "No. I just, I see stuff, and I think, she'd like that. That's it."

"I think that's just your love language," she said.

"My what?"

Marie looked up. "Love language. How people give or receive love. There's five. Gifts is one of them."

He laughed, then looked at her seriously. "So what's yours?"

Marie ran her fingers along the straps of the heels. "Words. Maybe time. It depends."

Bryson nodded slowly, like he was saving that for later. "Alright."

On Friday, Marie sat on the edge of Jaqueline's bed wearing a soft espresso-brown dress that was cinched at the waist. The hem floated just above her ankles showing off her gold strappy heels.

She opened her phone, thumbing through a few emails then stopping at the one she'd already read twenty times and still didn't quite believe it. The Fine Arts Collective was curating a show featuring emerging Black Southern artists—students, alumni, and professionals—and a professor had quietly submitted one of Marie's mixed media pieces.

The email was short but powerful:

We'd love to feature your work in the upcoming "Southern Visions" exhibition next semester. Let us know if you'd like to participate and if you have any other pieces you'd like us to consider.

Jaq would probably scream once she found out, and Marie wasn't quite ready for that yet. Not tonight, when her stomach was already fluttery about this mystery guy.

Jaqueline was checking herself in the mirror one last time. She wore a strapless black satin bustier with a wide-leg trouser that was tailored within an inch of it's life, and gold metallic Portofino heels.

She glanced at Marie from the mirror. "You look kind of nervous. You good?"

Marie smoothed the fabric over her hips. "It's been a minute since I did anything like this."

Jaqueline's brow lifted slightly. "Mm hmm."

Marie caught her tone in the reflection. "What?"

"You've been real... disciplined about sharing what's going on out in Atlanta," she said lightly, blotting her lip gloss. "No boys, no drama, no tea? You expect me to believe it's all books?"

Marie laughed under her breath. "It really is mostly books."

Jaq turned and crossed her arms. "So you mean to tell me, in a city full of fine Black men, and across the street from an all-male college, you're the only one that stayed celibate and stress-free?"

Marie kept her expression cool, but her ears warmed. Jaq knew she got shy around guys, especially without her there to break the ice like she always did.

She started to laugh it off, but Bryson's face flashed through her mind. The way he looked at her. The way it made her feel. She wished she could tell Jaq about it, but the words stuck in her throat.

She was afraid, afraid that saying it out loud might ruin the one friendship she couldn't stand to lose.

Jaqueline's eyes lingered a moment longer.

"Well," she said, "if anyone is blowing your back out, I just hope they're also bringing you coffee in the morning. That's the bare minimum."

Marie snorted, finally breaking. "You're ridiculous."

"I'm right," Jaq called as she grabbed her keys. "Come on girl. Let's go see what your date's hittin' for."

"What's his name again?" Marie asked.

Brandon's style leaned tailored. A man of pressed shirts, minimal jewelry, and shoes that looked expensive even when they weren't trying to be.

His fade was crisp, beard immaculate, and his confidence came from knowing where he came from and never pretending it wasn't a part of him.

At 23, he already ran his own logistics company. He started it off hustle and late nights in his cousin Tariq's garage mapping out their goals. Now, both their names sat on contracts that moved products through the Southeast.

The city stretched behind them in every direction as a soft playlist of R&B floated from the rooftop speakers.

The group had a cozy corner with a low table, string lights overhead, and candles flickering in recycled glass.

Jaq sat across from Tariq, stirring her peach lemonade slowly.

Tariq leaned toward her and asked, "So what got you into skincare? Like, what was the spark?"

Jaqueline half smiled. "Noticing what everyone else was doing wrong."

He laughed, clearly impressed. "That's a dangerous gift."

Meanwhile, at the opposite end of the table Brandon asked Marie, "You always this quiet, or am I just not interesting enough?"

Marie tilted her head, giving a lazy smile. "I'm not quiet. I'm just... observant."

He chuckled. "Alright, observant. What have you observed so far?"

Marie paused, thinking. She glanced at him, then away again, careful with her words.

"You iron your shirts and you seem…focused." she said slowly. "Like someone who doesn't move without purpose."

He tilted his head, considering that.

She gave a small shrug. "That's just my guess."

Tariq had just said something about holistic branding while Jaqueline sipped her drink smiling.

Brandon leaned back a little in his chair, watching Marie.

"So, how come someone like you is still single?"

Marie's fingers paused on her straw. "Someone like me?"

"You know what I mean," he said, "You're smart, funny, got your own thing going, pretty…and I mean that respectfully."

She gave him a raised brow and the smallest smirk. "Maybe I'm just not interested in distractions right now."

Jaqueline made a noise from the other side of the table— half a cough, half a laugh. Marie didn't look her way.

Brandon chuckled. "Okay, focus. I respect that. But like, no distractions ever?

Marie stirred her drink. "I think some people just… show up at the wrong time. Or maybe it's the right time, and you're just not ready."

His head tilted. "That sounds personal."

"It's not," she said.

Brandon smiled like he didn't believe her but wasn't gonna press. "I mean, I get it. It's hard out here."

"What about you?" she asked, changing the subject. "How come you're single?"

He stretched a little, glancing at the city skyline like it held the answer. "I've dated. I just got to a point where I didn't wanna be with somebody just to be with somebody, you know? I want someone who sees through all the performance."

Marie looked at him, then carefully asked. "And what do you usually perform?"

He laughed low. "That I'm fine all the time. That I know exactly what I'm doing. That I'm not still figuring things out."

Marie nodded. "Honest."

He tapped a finger against the table.

"I think most people are just pretending to have it together." Marie said softly.

Their eyes held a beat longer than expected.

Jaqueline's voice broke the moment.

"Valet's gonna be a mess if we wait any longer."

Brandon looked at Marie. "You riding with her?"

Jaq gave him a faux-sweet smile. "Yeah. She's with me."

Brandon laughed. "Just trying to walk her out like a gentleman."

She held up her hands. "Hey, I love a gentleman. Rare species these days."

Tariq and Jaq headed toward the elevators, leaving Brandon and Marie lingering behind.

"So," Brandon started, "I had a good time."

Marie gave a polite nod. "Yeah. Thanks for dinner."

"Can I get your number? Or do I have to take a quiz first?"

She smiled, almost apologetic. "I don't usually give my number out like that, but I'll take yours."

His brows lifted, just slightly.

He rattled off the digits, and she typed them in.

"I'll keep it respectful," he said as they walked slowly toward the elevators. "Maybe a good playlist if you're lucky."

Marie smiled. "I do judge people by their playlists."

They stepped into the elevator together, the doors sliding shut with a soft chime. The mirrored walls caught their reflections, making the space feel smaller than it was.

Brandon leaned against the rail, watching her with that easy confidence. "You know," he said, "you don't talk much, but it feels like you're saying more than most people."

Marie gave a soft laugh, eyes darting down to her heels.

"You've got plenty to say." he said smoothly. "You're just selective."

She felt her cheeks warm and hoped the dim golden light was enough to hide it.

The truth was, she was still thinking about Bryson, about the girls she'd heard whispers of. She'd never asked him if she was the only one. Maybe she was scared of the answer. Maybe she didn't want to know.

Brandon's gaze lingered, steady. "What?" she asked softly, finally meeting his eyes.

"Nothing," he said with a little grin. "Just glad I came out tonight."

The elevator hummed as it descended, her stomach fluttering in a way that wasn't entirely comfortable. Bryson was... Bryson, but he'd never actually said the words she wanted to hear. Never claimed her. Never made it official.

The elevator dinged, doors sliding open to the lobby. She slipped out first, keeping her pace steady. The air felt cooler down here, lighter somehow.

The valet stand buzzed with soft conversation and flashing taillights.

Jaq's Mercedes C200, rolled up first and Brandon opened the passenger door for Marie.

"Get home safe, alright?" he said, as Marie slid into the black leather seat.

She glanced back at him. "You too."

The ride home felt longer than the drive there. Marie leaned her head against the cool glass of the window, watching the lights blur past like they were in a hurry to get home too.

Jaqueline drove in silence for a while, one hand on the wheel, the other lazily flipping between tracks before settling on something slow.

"Okay, spill it," Jaq said, not even trying to be casual about it. "You like Brandon?"

Marie waited a beat too long.

"He was nice."

"Girl." Jaq gave Marie a look. "You just used the international word for 'I will never speak to that man again.'"

Marie smirked. "I'm just saying. He was cool, polite, drove a nice car, smelled good…"

"But?" Jaq interrupted.

Marie shrugged. "I wasn't even really there like that. I don't know."

The silence settled again. And then the storm.

"I know about you and my brother." Jaqueline said plainly. She didn't raise her voice, didn't even look at Marie, just dropped the words between them like something neither of them wanted to touch.

Marie didn't respond. She held her breath without really meaning to.

"I wasn't trying to be in your business," Jaq added. "Your phone was in the guest room the other night. I glanced and I saw the texts from him."

Marie's fingers curled around her clutch. She could feel her pulse in her ears.

"It wasn't supposed to be anything like that," she finally said, voice thin.

Jaqueline didn't look away from the road. "But it was, right?"

Marie stared out the passenger window. The strip mall passed in a blur. Her reflection in the glass looked distant.

"He didn't even ask me not to go tonight," she murmured, more to herself than anyone else.

She caught Jaq's profile in the glow of the dashboard. Her jaw was tight and that area just below her temple was doing that thing it did when she was holding something back.

"I'm not judging," Jaq said. Her tone was light, but there was weight under it, like a warning. "You're grown. I just hope you know what you're doing."

Marie didn't answer.

Jaqueline flicked the signal on. "Its wild how you used to act like love was a scam, and now..."

They pulled onto a quieter street, and Marie recognized the long curve of the road that led toward the lake. This was not the way home.

"You taking the long way?" She asked.

Jaqueline shrugged. "Thought you could use the air."

Marie nodded. That was the problem, though. The air. It was too still, too honest. It left nothing to hide behind.

"Jaq..."

"Don't."

The turn signal clicked steadily.

Click. Click. Click.

Marie's throat felt thick, tight. She didn't know what she was hoping for. Forgiveness? Permission?

The truth was, she hadn't been ready for any of it, not the way Bryson looked at her now, not the weight of hiding it from the one girl who'd always seen through her.

Jaqueline eased the car to a stop at the edge the lake. The engine ticked softly as it cooled.

Neither of them moved to get out.

Finally, Jaq spoke again, quiet but sharp enough to land. "He better not be playing you."

Marie didn't flinch and she didn't lie.

"I don't think he is."

Jaqueline sat with that for a moment, then she opened her door, stepped out, and shut it behind her without another word.

Marie stayed in the car, listening to the muffled sound of gravel under Jaqueline's heels as she disappeared into the night.

She told herself she wouldn't cry.

♪*Hound Dog* - Big Mama Thornton

8

The Girl Who Raised the Bar

♪ *How High is the Moon* - Ella Fitzgerald

"If you're not early, you're in the way."

That's what Mrs. Delilah Bell told the decorating crew as they rolled coolers and floral arrangements across her backyard at 7:08 a.m. One of them blinked like he was still half-asleep. She blinked back harder.

By 7:16, every table had been wiped down twice and the hydrangeas had been moved three times.

Chaos was for other people's houses, not hers.

She'd spent her teenage years inside of it, so much that she could still feel the scratch of borrowed heels that were always half a size too small.

When she turned sixteen, she'd promised herself two things: she would marry well, and she would never let her life be a mess someone else had to clean up.

Now here she was, curating brunch like it was the Essence Fest.

Delilah fluffed the hydrangeas on the tablescape, her mind still half-caught on the conversation she'd had with her son the night before.

Delilah was standing beside the fridge while Bryson raided it.

"I need you home tomorrow for brunch," she said casually.

He didn't even turn around. "Didn't know we were doing one."

"It's for family. A little get-together. Vanessa and her parents will be here also."

That made him pause.

He shut the fridge a little too hard for her liking.

"Don't start, Ma."

"I didn't say anything," she said, smiling into her wine glass. "You and Vanessa always had chemistry. You just never let yourself explore it. Might be time."

Bryson leaned on the counter opposite her now, jaw tight.

"What if I'm already seeing someone?"

She tilted her head, amused. "Are you?"

His silence was too quick to be innocent, too slow to be convincing.

"I didn't think so," she said before he could find an answer. "Besides, if you were serious about someone, I'd know. You'd bring her here. You'd want us to meet."

He didn't reply, just cracked his knuckles.

Delilah adjusted all of the centerpieces herself. She didn't trust the crew with symmetry. She didn't trust anyone with much of anything and she didn't need to. She'd built a life out of well-placed bets: on her career, her husband, her image.

Bryson would show up to the brunch. He always did, even if he didn't want to.

Vanessa would look beautiful. She always did, even when she pretended not to try.

And if the two of them just happened to reconnect in the soft afternoon glow, in front of God and her very tasteful brunch?

Well, that would just be good planning.

The sun showed up right on time, it's soft golden light spilling across the patio like she had sent for it herself. The tables were dressed in cream linens with gold chargers, tall glasses catching glints of morning light.

Vanessa showed up in a butter-yellow dress with her hair pulled back into a sleek ponytail that showed off her diamond studs. Her mother and father were behind her. One with a candle and the other holding a bottle of wine.

Delilah kissed her on both cheeks. "Don't you look radiant," she gushed, straightening Vanessa's necklace like a mother of the bride.

"Thanks," Vanessa said smiling.

From across the yard, Delilah caught a glimpse of Jaqueline and Bryson tucked off near the pool house, their voices too low to make out, but their faces loud with something unspoken.

Bryson looked every bit the boy who'd just gotten caught doing something. He also looked like he hadn't slept.

She'd ask about it later. Right now, the brunch still needed smiling through.

She excused herself and found her husband in the kitchen.

"You talked to your son lately?" she asked, light but direct.

He raised an eyebrow, "Just about everyday. Why?"

"He's off," she said. "Not rude. Just sideways."

Mr. Bell shrugged. "We were all sideways at his age."

Delilah folded her arms. "Has he said anything to you about a girl?"

"Not anything I'd repeat without backup."

He gave her the exact non-answer she expected. That irritated her. She hated when the men in her house played dumb and loyal.

She sighed. "Well, he needs to get clear. Vanessa is lovely. And she grew up around here. We know her people."

"I know you," Mr. Bell muttered, "You already got this girl mono-grammed into the towels."

Delilah smiled, but it didn't reach her eyes. "I just want what's best for him."

"You want what you can manage." he replied and walked off before she could snap back.

Delilah headed back out pretending to be focused on the charcuterie tray, but her eyes were tracking Bryson like a heat-seeking missile. He was making polite conversation with Vanessa's father, but he had the kind of body language she'd seen in boardrooms when a deal was going sideways.

When the guests had plates in hand and the playlist shifted to soft jazz, Delilah pulled Vanessa aside by the mimosa cart.

"You haven't spoken to Bryson yet?" she asked gently.

Vanessa blinked. "We spoke when I came in. That's about it."

Delilah frowned. "Go say more."

Vanessa looked unsure. "Mrs. Bell," she started. "I don't wanna seem like I'm chasing him."

"You're not. You're showing confidence. There's a difference."

Delilah rested a hand on her shoulder. "Sometimes men, even the good ones, need help seeing what's right in front of them. Just walk over, compliment his shirt, ask how school's going. Open the door. Let him walk through."

Vanessa nodded slowly, smoothing her dress. "Okay. Yeah. I can do that."

Delilah watched her walk away and for a split second, she saw herself at that same age. Pressed hair, pearl earrings, a skirt suit she borrowed from her older cousin. Back when she almost married a man named Sam. He loved her hard and loud, called her Dee-Dee and said he didn't need college or connections to build a life. He was going to open a tire shop.

Her mother had loved him.

She left Sam the summer after her sophomore year in college. That year she interned, where she met Mr. Bell. She'd chosen right. She just worried her mother never forgave her for it.

Delilah glided through her brunch, mimosa in hand. Compliments to every guest. Laughs that didn't wrinkle her forehead. A graceful pivot from every awkward pause.

Bryson was still drifting, but Delilah was patient. Plans didn't work because they were loud, they worked because they were consistent, and hers always were.

That last Saturday, she'd sent a text to Vanessa.

DELILAH: It was lovely seeing you this morning sweetheart. Hope your classes are treating you well. I forgot to ask and I know college can be a lot.

VANESSA: I had a good semester.

VANESSA: The weather was nice and campus has been peaceful mostly.

DELILAH: Mostly?

VANESSA: Nothing wild. Just a few surprises.

VANESSA: Ran into Bryson a couple times.

VANESSA: Didn't expect to see him with Jaqueline's friend.

DELILAH: Which friend?

VANESSA: I think her name's Marie? They seemed pretty close.

Delilah wasn't aware that they were spending time together away in Atlanta, but she also wasn't really all that surprised.

She'd seen it coming long before Vanessa said anything.

There was a summer, when the kids were in high school, Marie had stayed the weekend.

They were supposed to be watching a movie but Jaqueline was asleep on one end of the sectional and Bryson was stretched across the other end. Marie had fallen asleep in the middle, her head resting on Bryson's shoulder. He hadn't moved an inch. Not even when his arm went numb. Delilah remembered that part because she saw him shaking it out later.

And then, another night, she heard Marie whisper-laughing with him in the kitchen, asking him to pass her one of the leftover brownies.

There was something in the way they moved around each other.

It wasn't flirtation. It wasn't scandal. No it was worse. It was natural.

How his eyes instinctively found her in a room. How her shoulders dropped around him, just a little.

It was always small things. Small enough to ignore.

But Delilah Bell didn't ignore things.

She logged them, like a ledger. Now that the math was starting to add up, she didn't like the total one bit.

Marie's parents were probably too distracted to see it. That girl's been trying to build a home in someone else's house.

As the brunch began winding down, and guests started collecting their purses, Delilah surveyed her garden.

Everything looked perfect, but perfection was always an arrangement, not a truth.

Delilah learned that the hard way. From her mother, who told her that a woman only had so many choices before the world made them for her.

Mama always thought choosing right was about checking the right boxes. "I check mine with a pen, not a pencil." Delilah muttered to herself.

Now she had a daughter who barely looked her in the eye, a son who thought silence was protection, and a house full of decor hiding the real mess.

Still, Delilah smiled. She wasn't new to this.

She sipped her drink, let the last guests hug her goodbye, and said the thing she always said when her instincts were right and no one else knew yet:

"A storm always looks like it's skipping your house, right until it hits your porch."

When the house had settled again, the music was off, and the crew had started collecting their things, Delilah walked the upstairs with her heels dangling from two fingers.

She stopped at Jaqueline's door and knocked twice while pushing it open.

Her daughter sat on the bed, scrolling through her phone.

Delilah leaned against the dresser, arms folded. "What was that with you and your brother?"

Jaqueline's eyes flicked up, then back to her screen. "Nothing."

"You two don't look at each other like that over 'nothing.'"

Jaqueline set the phone down gently, like she was choosing patience. "Sometimes we just... talk sharp. But it's handled."

The tone was careful, even respectful. There was no eye-rolling, no smirks, but a wall in her daughter's voice that Delilah couldn't see past.

Delilah studied her. She was a gorgeous girl. Always had been. High cheekbones, long legs, deep-brown skin that glowed even without effort. She could walk into a room and every head would turn. Beauty, Delilah knew, was a double-edged sword. High maintenance, stubborn girls like that either built empires or burned bridges.

I had such high hopes for you, Delilah thought, before that night after one of Bryson's high school football games.

She could still see it—the bleachers emptying, her boy sweaty and beaming after another win, and Jaqueline slipping out. Delilah had gone looking for her, and there she was, pinned against a dented Buick, kissing some boy with gold teeth and sagging jeans. A boy who looked every inch the dope boy his grin promised.

Delilah had felt something inside her drop. Disappointment.

Delilah drew herself taller. "Your brother can't afford distractions right now. You saw how he was today…half here, half somewhere else."

Jaqueline didn't answer. She smoothed the edge of her skirt, a respectful silence hanging between them.

Delilah hated that silence almost more than defiance. It was harder to fight.

She wanted to shake her. To demand she explain herself. To ask what, exactly, she and Bryson had been whispering about during brunch.

But there was an order to these things. First, she had to secure Bryson. Secure the Bell name with Vanessa, with the right family, with the right future. After that, maybe she could work on Jaqueline, if it wasn't too late.

Delilah studied her another moment, searching her face for something.

Finally, she nodded once and left the room.

In her own suite, she shut the door, set her heels in their place, and sat at the vanity. Her reflection looked flawless: silk blouse, diamond necklace, lipstick still fresh. But beneath it, she could see the cracks.

Her son was distracted. Her daughter, stubborn. The ledger was off and Delilah never let the math stay wrong.

She picked up her phone, scrolled, and tapped a number she hadn't dialed in months.

When the line clicked open, she kept her voice light, almost sweet.

"Irma, I need a favor."

♪ *Ready or Not* - The Fugees

9

The Girl Who Raised Them

♪*Slip Away-* Clarence Carter

Mayfield stared down at blinking little square on the pool house door.

"Now what in the Sam Hill…" she muttered, jabbing her thumb at the sensor. The light flashed red again.

"I'll be," she said under her breath. "You need clearance to check on your own grandchild these days."

She jabbed the pad again, harder this time, as if showing it who was in charge.

From inside, she heard movement, then footsteps, and finally the door clicked open.

Bryson stood there, backlit by late afternoon light. "You good, Grandma?"

"No, I am not good," she said, brushing past him. "Thumbprint door locks."

Mayfield muttered as she sank onto the couch. She sat back and ran her hand along the armrest, the fabric stiff and too new. Everything in this house had been chosen by someone else, a decorator.

This wasn't her house, she never forgot that, still she'd spent more time here than most. When Jaq and Bryson were little and their parents were off catching flights and chasing promotions, it was Mayfield who came through that grand front door with a casserole in one hand and a switch in the other, just in case.

She remembered when Jaq lost her first tooth. She thought it was a disaster until Mayfield made a show of giving the tooth a nickname and putting it in an envelope under her pillow.

And Bryson? Lord. He used to crawl up into her lap with his plastic dinosaur he named Roary.

"You disappear like this after one of your mama's events," she said. "usually a sign you're either full or frustrated."

Bryson leaned against the wall for a second before slumping onto the love seat across from her.

He didn't speak right away. When he finally looked up, he asked, "You ever felt like your decisions were already made for you?"

Mayfield tilted her head. "You asking if I ever felt trapped? Baby, I'm a Black woman from the south born in 1942. We invented that feeling."

He cracked half a smile. "Right."

Bryson took in a breath. "I've never had time to figure out what I actually want."

He dropped his gaze.

"There's this girl…"

Mayfield said nothing.

"She's not the girl my mom wants," he added.

"Does she make you smile, even when you don't want to?" Mayfield asked.

He nodded. "Yeah."

"Well," Mayfield said, leaning back, "that's the kind that sticks."

Bryson rubbed his hands over his face. "She went on a date last night."

There it was. The crack in the mask.

"I knew she was going," he added quickly. "She told me. She was honest, but…"

"It still felt like a betrayal," Mayfield finished for him.

He didn't answer.

"You mad she went? Or mad you didn't ask her not to?"

He blinked, and for a second, looked every bit the little boy who used to sit on her front steps with skinned knees and 'squito bites.

Mayfield nodded. "Well, welcome to being grown."

Outside, the clean-up crew started rolling the trash bins down the driveway and someone was spraying down the patio.

"You think my Mama would ever accept her?" he asked, suddenly.

Mayfield gave him a look. "That's not the question. The question is, do you? And you don't have to answer me, baby. But you better be ready to answer yourself."

Her knees popped as she stood, brushing invisible lint from her skirt.

"Come see me next Sunday," she said gently. "I'll fry you up some fish and you can bring your lady-friend if you want."

Bryson smiled faintly. "Bet."

"Good. I'm taking my thumb back to where the doors open properly."

She winked and let the door shut behind her.

Bryson's words were still clinging to her, in that unsettling way where someone younger touches a nerve you thought you buried years ago. He hadn't meant to stir her like that. He was talking the way young folks talk, half-confident, half-searching, trying to carve sense out of the pieces of himself he didn't yet understand. And Lord, wasn't that familiar?

She wandered to the far edge of the property and found a bench. She sat slowly, knees aching, hands folded in her lap, and let herself drift.

She thought of Mississippi first.That red clay stuck to her bones, no matter how many children and grandchildren she'd watched scatter across the South.

She'd grown up in a shotgun house near Jackson, one of nine children, back when everything seemed louder — the crickets at night, the church bells on Sunday, even the griefs people carried. Back then, you couldn't hide your sorrow; it was always out on the porch, rocking in the chair beside you.

Her daddy was gone for work before the sun rose, home after it set. Her mama worked just as hard, though she never left the house. Mama's hands were always busy cooking, sewing, growing, plaiting. Mayfield had learned early what it meant to carry weight quietly.

So when Bryson sat in that pool house, shoulders heavy, talking about choices and losses and how tired he was already, it wasn't foreign to her. It was the same tune she'd been humming her whole life.

He thought the age gap made them different. She'd been through that storm before him, walked those same miles with shoes too thin.

She remembered seventeen, standing at the crossroads outside town with a boy who swore he'd marry her the second he scraped together enough to buy a ring. He had a smile that could split a storm, but he had nothing else. He wanted her to wait, to give herself over to a future that had no roof and no walls.

But she didn't.

At eighteen, she boarded a bus to Virginia with nothing but a suitcase. Virginia was where she learned the shape of her own loneliness.

She worked in a hotel laundry room, the steam pressing her skin damp every day, the white sheets never clean enough for the managers who barked orders in clipped tones.

She sent money home when she could, but mostly she kept it to herself, saving for things that mattered: a better pair of shoes, a dress that made her look like she had somewhere to go, a radio that could fill the room with music when the silence grew too sharp.

That's when she met Leonard.

Lord, Leonard.

He wasn't her first love, but he was the first man who looked at her like she was more than her circumstances. He played saxophone, his music always sliding like honey across the room.
He was taller than most, with a laugh that shook the table, and he carried himself like the world hadn't told him no yet. With him, she felt light, and free, and reckless enough to believe she could be somebody new.

They had a fire that burned quick and hot, the kind that leaves you dizzy. But Leonard wanted a life on the road, traveling with his horn. She wanted something steadier, like walls, doors, children who wouldn't wonder where their daddy had gone. So she let him go, even though her heart cracked with it.

She married Walter instead.

Walter was a church man, a man who worked for the post office and kept his shoes polished. He was safe, reliable, and he loved her in a way that didn't demand she set herself on fire.

With Walter, she built a life. They had children, Sunday dinners, a garden out back where she grew tomatoes and collards.

And still, sometimes, when the wind caught a certain tune, she wondered what she'd lost.

That was the thing Bryson didn't understand yet, how every choice you make leaves a ghost. You don't just live one life, you live with all the versions of yourself you might've been.

She wanted to tell him that the ache he felt at nineteen would still be there at seventy, only softer, folded into the fabric of who he was.

She leaned back on the bench, closing her eyes. She could almost smell the Mississippi clay, hear her mama calling her name from the porch.

Talking to Bryson was like talking to her younger self, the one who thought love could save her, or break her. The one who thought decisions were final, when really they just branched into more decisions.

She pressed her hands together, thumb rubbing over the ridge of her knuckle. Walter had been gone for years now, buried under an oak tree not far from here. She still spoke to him sometimes, in the quiet. She still told him things about the children, the grand-children. He would've been proud.

Maybe that was the real lesson she wanted Bryson to learn— that you don't escape your pain, but you can shape it into something that blesses somebody else.

Her throat tightened. She wished she'd said that to him in the pool house. But maybe he wouldn't have heard it anyway. You can't hear everything at once when you're young. Some truths only bloom with time.

She stayed there on the bench until the sun shifted. A breeze swept across her, carrying the faintest smell of barbecue from somewhere down the road, and she opened her eyes.

She wasn't sad, not exactly. Just full. Full of memories, of choices, of ghosts she'd learned to live with.

And as she rose, she thought, maybe she'd tell Bryson a story next time. Not advice, not warning, just a story. Because sometimes the only way to pass on wisdom is to let someone recognize themselves in your past.

She walked to her car slowly, ready to make her way back home.

She carried the pool house with her alongside Mississippi's red clay, Virginia's steam, and every ghost of the girl she once was.

♪ *In Due Time* – Outkast feat. Cee-Lo

10

The Girl Who Knew Too Much

♪ *What About Your Friends* - TLC

Jaq was wearing soft pajama pants that were loose and half-wrinkled from being curled up on the corner of the sectional too long. Her feet were bare, her edges had frizzed up, and she hadn't spoken to her brother since she nearly bit his head off at brunch yesterday.

She didn't feel guilty exactly.

But something about the way Bryson looked at her—surprised, like it was she who betrayed him—had stuck with her longer than she'd expected. Wasn't it time he felt something real? She'd played the role for years. The one who rebelled.

Her phone buzzed beside her.

TARIQ: Brandon hit me up. He will not stop talking about Marie.

JAQ: She does that to people.

TARIQ: He's respectful. But also like save her name as my emergency contact serious.

Jaqueline snorted.

JAQ: Tell him to please calm down.

It had been nearly 48hrs since Marie tried to explain away the situation with her and Bryson. They both knew it was messier than it should've been.

Marie hadn't reached out and Jaqueline hadn't either, but the silence, it wasn't sitting right.

She clicked open a new text and typed:

You free tomorrow? Thought we could go to the water park or something. Just us. You in?

She hit send and held her breath. Not because she didn't know what Marie would say, but because she wasn't even sure what she wanted.

She thought about her brother again.

About how he was probably holed up in the pool house, and how he'd looked at her like she'd exposed something ugly, when all she'd really done was remind him that he was playing both sides.

She wondered what her life would've looked like if she had just gone. Not to college, but anywhere. Somewhere she could start fresh without having to carry her family's ambition on her back.

Her phone buzzed again.

MARIE: Water park sounds like fun. I'm in.

Jaqueline exhaled. Tension she hadn't realized she was holding melted into the couch cushions.

Maybe they weren't fixed. But they were talking and that was something.

She sent one more message:

Cool. I'll pick you up.

She was barely off the phone when Bryson poked his head in.

"You look like you plotting something," he said, stepping into the living room.

"Let me guess, Vanessa said something slick at brunch and you're drafting your revenge?"

"Ha ha," she exaggerated, "Me and Marie are going to Wild Waves tomorrow. We need a break from everything."

He flopped into the armchair across from her "Oh, Wild Waves? Bet."

She blinked. "Bet what?"

"I'll come too."

"No," she said quickly.

"Yes," he said, "You know you can't swim. I might have to save your ass."

Jaqueline narrowed her eyes. "You don't even like water parks."

He smirked. "But I like Marie."

She threw a throw pillow at his face.

On Monday, they arrived at water park just before noon, the parking lot already teeming.

Jaqueline stepped out of her car like she was making a red carpet appearance in a black one-piece, shorts, and breezy kimono. It was the kind of outfit meant to stand next to water, not get in it.

Marie looked summery in a tan high-waisted bikini, throwback Grays jersey for a cover-up, Birkenstock's, and her cat-eye shades.

Bryson rolled up unapologetically minutes after them, in black trunks, a fresh white tank, and the same gold chain he always wore.

Jaq watched as Marie glanced at him quickly and then looked away.

Bryson nodded at them like this wasn't weird.

"So," he said, "whats first? Lazy river or go straight for the slides?"

"No one invited you," Jaqueline muttered.

Marie gave a polite laugh that could have passed for a cough.

They got in line for wristbands. Bryson paid for Jaqueline's, and tried to pay for Marie's but she declined.

"Don't be weird," he told her.

They walked through the turnstile and into a burst of chlorine-scented air. The place buzzed with kids shrieking near the splash pad, lifeguards blowing whistles, and the constant slosh of water against concrete.

They wandered past a food stand advertising funnel cakes and frozen lemonades. Bryson bought one of each, declaring he couldn't choose, then handed Marie the lemonade without asking if she wanted it. Jaqueline peeled off toward the lockers, forcing Marie and Bryson into a lopsided walk together.

Marie sipped the lemonade as Bryson kept pointing out rides trying to get her to agree to one of the big slides.

When Jaq rejoined them, they all agreed on "starting slow" on the lazy river.

The three of them drifted side by side in brightly colored tubes, the current carrying them past fake boulders and palm trees that looked more plastic than alive. Sunlight flickered on the water, warm on their faces, almost enough to trick someone into thinking this was peaceful.

Marie floated with her head tipped back, sunglasses hiding her eyes. She barely moved, her fingers trailing through the water.

Jaqueline was doing her best imitation of carefree. She was leaned back, chin high, spinning lazily in her tube whenever the current allowed, until Bryson sent a sharp splash across her shoulder.

"Wow. Grown man behavior," she said, wiping at her cheek with the heel of her hand, pressing down the urge to flip his tube.

Bryson grinned, unbothered.

Marie laughed a short burst that must've surprised even her, but it caught in her throat, turning into a cough she tried to wave off. She went quiet again, adjusting her sunglasses, letting the sound of the water swallow whatever expression she might have had.

She let the current pull her just slightly ahead, giving herself space, but she could hear them talking behind her. Bryson's voice was dipping into that low, easy tone, Marie answering soft, like she didn't want to be overheard.

She dipped her hand into the water, flicked it aimlessly, pretending she wasn't listening. Pretending she didn't notice their knees brushing every few seconds with the shift of the current.

When they got off the river and walked to the wave pool, Jaq pretended she needed to hang back at the picnic tables and check her phone so she wouldn't have to referee whatever energy was simmering between the two of them.

She opened her messages with Tariq.

JAQ: Hope Brandon hasn't started naming their kids yet. He's sweet, but I don't think Marie's interested.

TARIQ: Copy that. I'll let him know. He'll survive probably.

She huffed out a quiet laugh and slid her phone face down on the towel beside her. The sun was hot on her skin, and somewhere across the park, she could hear the mechanical groan of the wave pool starting up.

She looked up to see Marie and Bryson orbiting each other like broken magnets. Then they both started toward her, Bryson with a grin.

"The big slides?" he challenged as he approached the picnic table.

Marie's smile was thin. "I'll pass."

"C'mon, it's basically law," Bryson said. "You can't come here and not hit the slides."

Jaq raised an eyebrow. "Who exactly enforces this law?"

"Me," he said, already walking backward toward the stairs.

She wasn't about to admit it, but she'd been eyeing that ridiculous neon tangle of fiberglass.

"Fine," she said, standing and stretching.

The climb up the stairs was brutal and the railing was scorching hot. Bryson kept glancing over his shoulder with a smirk, so she decided she'd take that as motivation to beat him down the slide.

At the top, the view stretched out over the whole park. Marie gave them a wave from below. "Ready to lose?" Bryson asked.

Jaq rolled her eyes and dropped into her lane, hands gripping the slick sides. A whistle blew. She shoved off hard.

The afternoon stretched long and heavy.

By the time they headed back to the car, they smelled like chlorine and fried food.

As soon as she got home Jaqueline took off her lashes, showered, wrapped her hair, then curled back up in her spot on the couch with a cup of tea she wasn't drinking.

Bryson walked in with that same quiet confidence that used to charm her, back before she knew how careless he could be with people's hearts.

She didn't look up.

"You good?" he asked finally.

"Define good."

She reached for the remote and then changed her mind. "Look, I'm not trying to be in you and Marie's business anymore."

He crossed his arms. "Could've fooled me."

"She's not built like me," Jaqueline said. "You break her, it's not just a mess. It's damage."

He nodded slowly. "She told me about the date."

Jaq turned her head toward him now.

"Did that make you feel better?"

"I don't know what I feel." He rubbed the back of his neck. "Like I had all this time to do something, and I didn't."

Jaq finally sipped her tea.

"I actually came to tell you something." He said.

She stared at him blinking slow. "You pregnant?"

He didn't smile. Not even a twitch.

"Dad pulled me aside said I should be careful." Bryson shifted, arms crossed tight.

She leaned forward, voice sharp. "Careful how?"

Bryson looked away for a second, then back at her. "Careful about Mom. He said she's got a some type of plan. Been having conversations behind my back."

Her jaw tightened. "Conversations like what?"

Bryson hesitated, then gave her that you're-not-gonna-like-this look. "He said she already talked to Vanessa and her parents about long-term goals. Said she's keeping an eye on me...and Marie."

Jaqueline didn't respond at first. Just stared at him, lips parted, heart pacing faster than she wanted to admit.

"She's keeping an eye on you... and Marie?" she repeated, slower, like she needed to hear it out loud again.

"Guess he figured it's better I hear it from him than find out after Mom goes full Olivia Pope."

Jaq blinked. "Wait. How does she even know about you and Marie?"

Bryson leaned back, rubbing a hand over his face. "Your guess is as good as mine. She just knows. Like she always does."

Jaqueline narrowed her eyes. "Knows what, exactly? You never really laid it all out for me."

Bryson hesitated, then sighed. "That Marie... means something to me."

He finally looked up, straight at her. "I got an apartment off-campus."

Jaqueline's brows shot up. "Excuse me?"

"Most days we cook together, do homework..." he explained.

Jaqueline just stared, lips slightly parted. "You've been playing house, while Mom's been playing chess."

He chuckled under his breath. "Jaq, I didn't plan for it to get this serious with Marie. It just did."

She paused, "You love her?"

"Yeah," he said without blinking. "I do."

"You told her that?"

"Not in those words," he said, "but I think she knows."

She crossed her arms. "So what now?

"I've never had to stand up to Ma before," he said "But I will."

Jaqueline studied him."Well, it's about time"

She let out a long exhale. "We need a family meeting."

"No," Bryson said. "We need a war plan."

♪ *Outkast* - B.O.B

11

The Girl Who Worried

♪ *Choppa Style* -Choppa

Renae was in the kitchen chopping cucumbers for a pasta salad when Marie came home, smelling like heat and chlorine.

The screen door creaked and slapped shut, then Marie's shadow fell long across the linoleum. She had that heavy, slow walk she always did when her head was full.

"Hey, Ma," she said, grabbing the fridge handle without looking around.

The rhythmic thock-thock-thock of the knife filled the space between them. She didn't turn yet, just slid the neat half-moons into the bowl, her eyes steady on the cutting board.

"How was the water park?"

Marie pulled out the lemonade, the one with her name on it in Sharpie.

"Loud. Wet. Full of kids." Marie tilted the bottle to her mouth.

"So, good'?" Renae asked, smirking.

Marie smiled, swallowing hard. "It was fine. Jaq and I needed a day out."

Renae didn't ask who else was there. She knew better. Sometimes silence got you further than a dozen questions. She rinsed her knife under the faucet, let the water run over her hands longer than she needed to, then turned.

"You being safe out here, right Marie?"

Marie's eyes flicked up. "That's random."

"Not really. You said you and Jaq had a double-date the other night."

That word "date" hung in the air too long. It was soft but sharp, like a thorn wrapped in tissue paper. Marie set the lemonade down on the counter with a little more force than she meant to.

"Safe how?" she asked, though she already knew.

Renae sighed, pulling a dish towel from the oven handle and drying her hands. She walked slower now, like she was moving toward something fragile.

"Safe in every way," she said. "Your heart, your name. I just need to know you're thinking about your future. You've worked too hard to let anything take that away."

Marie said nothing. She fiddled with the bottle cap, twisting it open and shut, her lips pressed tight.

"I'm not judging you," Renae added quickly. She hated that silence could sometimes feel like a verdict. "I just... I need to be sure you're guarding yourself. This world is not soft on Black girls with ambition. It'll clap for you one day and trip you the next."

Marie exhaled hard through her nose. "I know. I promise I know."

Renae's face softened. That was the thing with her daughter, some-times the quiet words were the most honest.

She reached across the counter, brushed Marie's hand with her fingertips before pulling back. "You're my only one, Marie."

Marie cracked a smile, shaking her head.

Renae laughed, reached for the wooden spoon to stir the pasta salad. The sound loosened the air again, made the kitchen feel more like a home and less like a courtroom.

Her husband poked his head into the kitchen just long enough to raise an eyebrow at Marie. He smelled faintly of motor oil, like he'd been tinkering with something.

"I got a shovel and a quiet backyard," he said with a wink.

Marie rolled her eyes so hard they might've touched the back of her skull. "Oh my God."

"I'm just sayin'." He shrugged, vanishing back into the den, the floor creaking beneath his retreat.

Renae stirred the pasta salad, and for a moment her mind slipped years back, to the night she wasn't even supposed to be out.

Her mama had warned her about places like that — low ceilings, liquor-sticky floors, women in heels too high. After the week she'd had at work, after all the prayers and pretending, Renae needed something with a pulse.

She let her cousin Yvonne drag her to Red Velvet Lounge, a blink-and-you'll-miss-it spot off the county road that stayed packed with regulars and trouble alike.

She was on her second glass of Crown and ginger when he walked in.

Not loud, not looking around for attention like half the men in there. Just tall and steady, in a short-sleeved button-down that clung to his arms. He had a walk like he wasn't in a rush to impress nobody, and that made him even harder to ignore.

"You see that?" Yvonne elbowed her.

"I see a man minding his business," Renae said. But she kept watching.

He didn't head for the bar. Didn't try to dance. Just stood near the stage, nodding along as the singer belted out a cover of "Ain't No Way," eyes closed like she meant it from the bottom of her bones.

That's when he glanced Renae's way and smiled.

129

Not one of those full-lipped, hey-girl-I-see-you kind of smiles. Just a slow, polite stretch of the mouth, like he saw something familiar in her face and wanted her to know it.

She looked away fast, heat flashing under her collar.

Five minutes later, he was sliding into the seat across from her like he'd been invited. Like it was the most natural thing in the world.

"You don't look like you come here often," he said.

"You don't either."

He shrugged. "I come for the music."

They talked.

And that's all it was at first, just talking. No smooth pickup lines, no leaning in too close. He asked about her job, about her folks. Told her he worked with his hands — carpentry, mostly, but whatever paid.

"You build things?" she asked, sipping slow.

"I try to," he said. "Fix 'em too. Not everything that breaks needs to be thrown out."

She blinked. Something about the way he said it stuck with her.

They danced one time before she left. Slow two-step. Nothing fancy. He didn't press his body to hers, just kept one respectful hand at the small of her back and moved like the music was meant for them.

Outside, he walked her to her car. He didn't ask for her number.

"You coming back next Friday?" he asked instead.

She didn't answer right away. Just unlocked her door and turned to look at him, lit by the red neon bouncing off the roof of the club.

"I might."

"Good," he said. "I'll save you a seat."

That was the thing about him. He didn't push. He didn't beg. He just stayed, like a nail driven deep, like a beam holding up more than it looked like it could.

They dated for a year and some change. Friday nights at Red Velvet turned into Saturday mornings in her kitchen, him helping her flip pancakes in his undershirt. They talked about a future, houses and babies and porch swings, but always like they had time.

Renae found out she was pregnant two weeks after her 24th birthday. She hadn't planned it, but the second that little pink line darkened, her whole world tilted toward motherhood like it was where she was always headed.

"You're sure?" he had asked, eyes locked on hers.

"I took three tests."

He nodded, then pulled her in. "Well," he murmured, lips in her hair. "Looks like we're gonna need more pancakes."

131

They started planning, not a wedding, but a nursery. A crib he swore he'd build himself, paint swatches taped to the wall. Her body aching in strange new ways, like the world inside her was stretching, rearranging.

But then it stopped. She started spotting. She told herself it was normal, that it could be normal. But in her gut, she knew it wasn't.

He went with her to the doctor. No heartbeat.

She didn't cry, not at first, she just folded in on herself and didn't say much for days. She didn't go back to work, she didn't answer Yvonne's calls, she just sat on the couch with a blanket across her lap like grief was something she had to keep warm.

He cooked. He cleaned. He ran a bath when she wouldn't. One night, he didn't say anything, just sat beside her and picked up her foot, rubbing slow circles into her arch until she finally broke down.

"I never even got to hear the heartbeat," she sobbed. "I was gonna be somebody's mama."

"You are," he said. "That baby was real. Just... didn't get to stay long."

They didn't talk about marriage again for months. Then one Sunday morning, Renae came into the kitchen to find him fixing the leaky sink, humming something soft and gospel. The light was slanting in through the window just right, hitting the side of his face.

"You wanna go to the courthouse tomorrow?" she asked, leaning on the door frame.

He paused mid-turn of the wrench, head cocked. "Is that a proposal?"

"It's a yes or no question."

He grinned, that same quiet stretch of mouth from the night they met.

"Yeah," he said. "But I still want to get you a ring."

Renae gave a small smile, the kind that stayed mostly in the eyes. "You can get me a ring after. Right now I just want your name."

He wiped his hands on a rag and stood.

"You sure you don't want anything fancy?" he asked. "Cake? Dress? Something you can show off later when the kids ask how we did it?"

"We've been doing it," she said. "This is just paperwork to catch up."

He stepped closer, and without the grease and sweat and time between them, it might've looked like a movie moment. But this was better, realer.

"Alright then," he said. "Tomorrow. I'll even wear my good shoes."

♪ *Do Right Man* —Aretha Franklin

12

The Girl Who Pulled Strings

♪*Rockin' That Shit* - The Dream

Delilah Bell never let the heat get to her, at least not visibly. She lounged in the private spa suite at The Stillwater, a tucked-away secret for quiet women with loud bank accounts.

Across from her, Vanessa wore the same gray robe, feet soaking in a citrus bath while a tech buffed her nails.

"Its so quiet here." Vanessa said, letting her head tilt back against the rolled towel.

Delilah smiled without smiling. "Silence is the luxury most people can't afford."

Vanessa chuckled lightly, unsure whether to take it as wisdom or warning. "So," she began, "you were telling me about Bryson's birthday."

Delilah nodded, like she'd been waiting. "We're doing a yacht party. Something polished. Clean lines. That end-of-summer kind of glow."

"Will it be just family?" Vanessa asked casually, trying not to sound too invested.

"Oh, it'll feel that way," Delilah replied, waving her hand. "A curated crowd. College friends. A few family associates."

Vanessa nodded. She'd learned early not to ask too many follow-ups.

"I've already spoken to the chef. Light fare. Cocktail service. Good music. It's not just a party. People should know what kind of man Bryson is becoming."

Vanessa dipped her foot deeper into the warm water. "And I guess you've got... everything else figured out?"

Delilah turned her head slightly and looked at Vanessa without blinking. "Of course."

Vanessa looked relieved. "Good. I just want it to be special for him."

Delilah reached for her glass of cucumber water and took a measured sip. "It will be."

She set the glass down with care. "I know what I'm doing, Vanessa. You don't need to worry about her. Or anyone else."

Vanessa nodded again, silent.

"And when you walk into that party, I want you to walk like you know you belong beside him. Not behind. Not beneath. Beside."

Vanessa swallowed, a mix of flattery and pressure sitting at the base of her throat.

Delilah leaned back again, her tone lighter. "Besides, it's not about the girl. It's about the path."

"And you've mapped it already," Vanessa said, trying to sound breezy.

Delilah's smile returned, this time a little fuller. "I've had the map drawn since before Bryson could drive."

And with that, the spa door eased open and an attendant stepped in with fresh towels and a reminder of their next treatment. Delilah didn't move yet. She stayed behind a second longer, just long enough to close her eyes and breathe in the stillness. Everything was falling into place.

You didn't throw a party just to throw a party. You built a moment, shaped it, polished it, gave it meaning. That was the difference between a good mother and an ordinary one. The ordinary ones just showed up. The good ones? They arranged the stage.

And right now, her son was the leading man.

She texted him.

You free to talk? Need a few minutes about your birthday.

His reply came minutes later. Short and neutral, as always.

Yup. I'm home.

She didn't bother responding. Knew better than to have this conversation over the phone. She wanted to see his face.

When their treatments ended, Delilah didn't linger. She slipped behind the wheel of her Mercedes S550, the leather still warm from the sun, and called her sister on speaker as she eased out of the lot.

"Dee? You alive?" Sharon's voice was warm, teasing.

"Barely," Delilah said with a smile. "I'm running around like I'm the one turning twenty."

"You love it. Don't lie."

Delilah chuckled, low and smooth. "Maybe I do. But it's more than a party. You know that."

"Always is, with you." Sharon sighed. "Don't wear yourself down."

Delilah didn't respond. She slid into traffic, skyscrapers giving way to low houses and tidy lawns. She thought of Bryson at seven, running full tilt across the yard, his laughter loud enough to startle the birds from the trees. He'd always had that shine, that pull. People looked at him and wanted to follow.

Her sister broke the silence. "So how's he doing, really? Happy? Focused?"

Delilah considered the question. "He's... steady. Not where he should be, but not lost either. He's learning."

"Learning what?"

"How to carry a name."

Sharon laughed softly. "You make it sound like a crown."

"It is," Delilah said. "And you know crowns aren't light."

There was a pause, then Sharon said gently, "Don't squeeze him too hard."

Delilah's eyes narrowed, though not at her sister. She was watching a group of boys on the corner, loud, careless, their futures leaking away in laughter and smoke. "Better I squeeze than the world crush him. He'll thank me later."

She ended the call before Sharon could argue.

The car eased into her driveway. The gardenias were in bloom, their sweetness curling in the air. Delilah paused before going inside, her fingers brushing the petals.

She made a mental note: flowers for the yacht. Lots of them.

When she finally stepped into the house, the cool air wrapped around her shoulders, and the faint hum of Bryson's music drifted from the backyard. Her lips curved in the kind of smile that wasn't quite joy, but something close.

Everything was moving. Everything was aligning.

Bryson was pool-side, lounging with his tablet in one hand and an apple in the other.

"Hey," he mumbled around a bite.

"Hey yourself," she said, kissing the top of his head like he was still seven. "You busy?"

He lifted one brow.

She smiled and sat across from him. "So. Twenty. That's not a little-boy anymore."

He gave a small shrug. "It's just another number."

"It's not. After this, you are officially a man. You're not a teen anymore. You know what that means?"

"That you're gonna throw me a party no matter what I say?" Bryson asked.

Delilah laughed. "Correct."

Bryson looked amused, but tired, the way he always did when he knew he wasn't going to win but still went through the motions. "I told you I didn't want anything crazy."

"And I listened," she said. "I reserved a private yacht. Simple. Elegant. Just family and close friends. Vanessa helped me brainstorm."

The second her name hit the air, she saw it. That flicker, like a match being snuffed, right in his jaw.

"Ma," he said.

Delilah tilted her head. "Look, baby. I know you been doing your own thing, and I respect it. But you only turn twenty once. Let your mama celebrate you the right way."

He didn't say anything for a moment.

"You can bring someone," she added. "If there's someone worth bringing."

She stood, not waiting for his answer.

"Let me know by next week. I need the final headcount by Tuesday."

She started to leave but paused in the doorway, her voice lighter this time.

"You know, Bryson, you can trust me. I only want what's best for you."

He didn't respond. Just looked down at his tablet. She grabbed her keys.

Delilah Bell didn't like to keep people waiting, but she didn't rush either. She drove in silence, the world outside carefully tuned out. Forty-five minutes later, she turned onto a sleepy side street.

The building didn't have a sign. It never had. But everyone who mattered knew it.

She parked and stepped inside. It smelled of cedar.

Miss Irma, who'd been working under a bare bulb, didn't look up. She simply said, "You're late."

Delilah didn't take offense. Irma was old as folk and twice as sharp. You didn't come here for kindness. You came for results.

"I need two things," Delilah said, unclasping her purse and placing two fine linen garment bags on the counter. "His suit and her dress."

Irma looked up then, her eyes bright behind gold-rimmed glasses. "The same girl?"

Delilah's mouth twitched. "No. The right one this time."

Irma reached for the bag with long, practiced fingers and unzipped the first. It was a crisp navy suit, Italian, double-breasted.

Irma nodded, as though she'd been expecting this. "You're playing with big energy."

Delilah met her eyes. "I'm protecting my son's future."

Irma didn't argue. She simply pulled a small carved box from beneath the worktable and placed it beside the suit.

Inside: black thread dipped in oil, fine silver needles, and a slip of parchment worn from time .

"Two garments," Irma said. "Same frequency?"

Delilah replied. "I want him clear. I want her soft."

Irma hummed, not with judgment, but with recognition. "You're going to owe me a favor."

"I always pay my debts," Delilah said. She pulled out a thick envelope and placed it on the table. "Half now. Half when it's done."

Irma didn't touch the money. She only nodded. "Come back next week. They'll be ready."

Delilah turned to go, then paused at the door. "And Irma, make sure the seams are clean."
Irma smiled to herself. "I never sew sloppy, sugar."

Delilah drove home slowly, letting the weight of what she'd set in motion sit with her. Everything would look effortless, like it always did. The cake would be perfect. The speeches short. The guest list elite. And when Bryson stood beside Vanessa, he'd feel it. He wouldn't know why, but he would.

♪ *Blackwater Blues* - Bessie Smith

13

The Girl Who Saw the Sign

♪ *Grown Woman* - Beyonce

Jaqueline eased her Mercedes to a stop in front of the tidy brick house, the engine purring into silence. She sat there a moment, phone balanced on the steering wheel, scrolling through unread texts with one perfectly manicured nail.

There was the tray of coffees on the passenger seat from the little boutique café that charged an arm and a leg for an iced latte just because they could.

She adjusted her sunglasses in the mirror, reapplied gloss in one precise swipe, then she took a deep breath, picked up the coffee carrier, and stepped out of the car.

The air was hot and sticky, but Jaqueline's stride was cool, always. She rang the doorbell once, shifting her weight on the porch while glancing at her reflection in the glass.

The door opened, and Marie's mom stood there in a floral robe, eyebrows raised.

"Jaqueline," she said, a little surprised, a little amused. "Well, don't you look like a model."

Jaq leaned in with a quick hug, careful not to spill the coffees. "I try. Got us all something from Juno's. They finally got that lavender oat milk back in stock."

"That place with the line down the block?" Marie's mom said, her tone playful but impressed.

"Only took me twenty minutes this time," Jaq said with mock exasperation. "But it's worth it."

Marie's mom chuckled, shaking her head. "You young folk and your fancy drinks. Back in my day, we just drank Folgers and got on with it."

Jaqueline smiled sweetly. "Marie and I need fuel, we've got work to do."

Marie's mother eyed her knowingly. "Mm-hmm. Well, she's in her room. Don't let her hole up too long. She forgets to eat when she gets in her zone."

"She won't forget with me here," Jaqueline promised, handing her a latte and stepping past with the coffee carrier in tow.

The house smelled faintly of lemon polish and fried chicken, layered with the comforting undertone of home. Her heels clicked softly against the hardwood as she made her way up the hall. She passed the familiar gallery of framed school pictures and family portraits, pausing for just half a second at the one of Marie in her cap and gown.

Reaching Marie's door, she shifted the coffees to one hand and knocked lightly before pushing it open without waiting for an answer.

"I brought coffee," she announced, sweeping into the room, sunglasses still on, bag swinging dramatically from her shoulder.

Marie arched a brow. "We designing your pop-up or doing a photo shoot?"

Jaqueline dropped her bag dramatically onto Marie's bed. "Both. You never know when inspiration hits."

Marie grinned. "Well, I've been thinking, you should do something that says luxury, limited, but a little bit unbothered."

"You basically just described me," Jaq laughed. "See, that's why I trust you."

As she described her vision, Marie started sketching loose lines that hinted at something bold but feminine.

"How do you feel about incorporating some brown?" Marie asked.

Jaqueline's eyes wandered and landed on the Louis duffle that was tucked beneath Marie's desk. She leaned and pulled it out.

Marie smiled. "The Louis color palette definitely screams luxury. I can make that work."

She unzipped the side pocket casually. Her fingers brushed the interior lining, pausing as she noticed a tiny stitch she hadn't remembered seeing before. It wasn't just a stitch. It was a symbol.

Small, barely there, tucked into the seam like it was never meant to be found.

Jaqueline leaned in closer, squinting. "Okay, what is this?"

Marie turned, puzzled. "What's what?"

"There's like, a weird little symbol inside the lining. Right here." She held it open for Marie to see.

Marie came over and peered inside. The mark was maybe half an inch wide. Some sort of looping design. It was not quite a letter, but not really a shape either.

Jaqueline's voice was flat. "Did you get your bag blessed or something?"

"Wow. Dramatic." Marie gave her a look, part amused, part exhausted.

"I'm just saying, If I find out this bag's got y'all soul-tied, I'm burning it."

Jaq zipped the bag shut and slid it to the edge of the bed. "Speaking of energy, I need to get mine right. I've got a plans tonight. Dinner with Tariq."

Marie raised an eyebrow. "Oh? Just the two of y'all?"

Jaqueline grinned. "Just the two of us."

Marie smirked. "You mean, you didn't get all cleaned up just to boss me around?"

Jaq tossed her hair over her shoulder. "Multitasking," she said, flashing a grin as she spritzed perfume at her pulse points—neck, wrists, behind the knees.

"Where are y'all going?" Marie asked, closing up her laptop.

"Sushi spot. And let's just say, I'm not above letting his hand 'accidentally' land somewhere it's been thinking about."

Marie gasped, grinning. "You did *not* just say that."

"I'm just saying!" Jaqueline shrugged innocently. "It's dinner, but if dessert is served, I'm not skipping."

Marie laughed. "Okay, poetic! Be safe."

"I always am," Jaqueline said, "And it's not like I'm tryna rush anything, but he smells good, he listens. And when he talks to me, he talks like I'm a person. Not a challenge. Not a prize."

Marie smiled at that. "I hear you."

"It's been a minute since I wanted to lean in. "But this feels different. Grown," Jaqueline said, assessing her edges in the mirror.

147

Marie smiled. "Well, I'm happy for you."

Jaqueline caught her eyes in the reflection and held the look a little too long.

Then she turned slowly. "Speaking of grown. We gonna talk about you and my brother now, or are we gonna keep pretending I don't know?"

Marie tried to recover with a light scoff, reaching for a bottle of lotion she didn't need.

Jaq tilted her head, unimpressed. "Girl, stop. Go ahead. Say *something.*"

Marie sighed, slowly pressing the bottle closed. The silence stretched between them like fabric she didn't know how to fold.

"It really did start off as nothing." Marie said.

Jaqueline tilted her head.

Marie met her gaze and said, "I didn't plan it, but I'm not gonna stand here and act like it wasn't real, like it still isn't."

Jaq blinked, caught off guard by the quiet conviction in her voice. This wasn't guilt or defiance. It was just Marie, standing in the middle of the truth.

"I'm not sorry for how I feel about him," Marie added. "But I do apologize for not trusting you with it. That's on me."

"You know what hurts the most?" Jaqueline crossed her arms, torn between admiration and frustration. "I had your back. Always. And y'all acted like I was the one you had to work around."

Marie didn't flinch. "We didn't want to work around you. We just didn't know what we were doing yet. I wasn't about to put you in the middle of something half-formed."

Jaq sat with that, letting it settle.

She could still feel the sting of betrayal, but now it was braided with something else, reluctant respect. Marie wasn't hiding anymore, and she wasn't begging, either.

Jaqueline exhaled through her nose, the tension loosening. "You're still shady for not telling me."

"You love me anyway?" Marie asked.

Jaqueline side-eyed her. "Barely."

Marie smiled. "I'll take it."

They sat like that for a second, somewhere between the beginning and the rebuild.

Jaqueline didn't say she was over it. Because she wasn't.

Marie shook her head, "Go get your man, Jaq."

"I fully intend to," Jaqueline said, already grabbing her keys.

She had worn black, of course. A black silk slip, cropped blazer hanging off her shoulders, and subtle gold hoops.

Tariq was already at the table when she arrived. Button-down open just enough, rings on both hands, that slow smirk that made it hard to stay mad at anything for too long.

"You clean up nice," he said, standing as she approached.

"And you're still talking shit," she replied, sliding into her seat with a sigh. "God really did give his smartest mouth to his prettiest ones."

He laughed, then leaned in. "You good though?"

She didn't respond right away. The waiter brought water, took their orders, then disappeared.

Finally, she said, "You ever find out your best friend was sneaking around with your brother?"

Tariq blinked. "Marie? Straight like that?"

She sipped her water. "No chaser."

He tilted his head.

"Thing is, my mom's got this whole little fairy tale planned for my brother."

"Lemme guess, your best friend wasn't cast in the original?"

"Nope," Jaqueline said, shaking her head. "It's like she made this alternate life for him and is just waiting for it to become reality."

Tariq leaned back. "That sounds…familiar."

She raised a brow.

"My pops used to push me real hard to go into real estate. His thing was, if you can't be famous, at least you can own what people care about. But I wasn't tryna be another version of him."

"What would you do? If you were me?" She asked.

"So if my sibling and my friend were kissing behind my back while my mom planned his engagement to someone else?"

"Exactly that."

Tariq paused, serious now. "I'd stay out of it. If you step in it too deep, you either end up heartbroken, hated, or held responsible."

Jaqueline frowned.

"But," he added, "I would check in with my people. Let them know the silence hurts more than the truth ever could."

She stared at him for a moment. "You're smarter than you look."

"I get that a lot."

Jaqueline toyed with her chopsticks as the waiter set their plates in front of them.

"Thanks for listening," she said, quietly. "I didn't realize how heavy it all felt until I said it all out loud."

"That's what I'm here for," Tariq said. "Well that, and dessert."

She rolled her eyes, but she wasn't frowning anymore.

Jaqueline wiped her mouth delicately with the linen napkin, side-eyeing Tariq as he tapped his phone screen with an obnoxious little grin.

"You texting someone fun?"

He looked up like a kid caught mid-prank. "Actually, Brandon."

"Really?" She tilted her head.

"He's still a little bummed but said something about how he thought Marie seemed unreachable at dinner that night. But, not in a snobby way."

"Marie has always been that way," she murmured. "She lets you in just enough to make you think she trusts you, but there's always this little door she keeps locked."

Tariq raised a brow. "You mad she kept it locked from you?"

She looked away. "I'm mad she gave my brother the key."

They sat with it a moment, letting the music swell and the air between them.

"You ever thought about moving?" he asked. "Getting some space from… all that?"

Jaqueline huffed a dry laugh. "Every week since I turned eighteen. But my business runs out of that house. My mama's strings don't cut easy."

Tariq smiled. "I got scissors."

She rolled her eyes, laughing softly as she turned away.

Then, as if remembering something, Tariq reached into his shirt pocket and pulled out a slim, gold matchbook. It was worn smooth at the edges, but clearly something special.

Embossed on the front was a single rose.

He handed it to her without a word.

Jaqueline turned it over in her palm, eyebrows lifting. "This is… kind of beautiful."

"Found it at a flea market," he said. "Vendor didn't know where it was from it just looked… romantic."

She gave him a sideways look. "And you thought of me?"

He shrugged, like it wasn't a big deal. "Low key, kind of sharp, pretty without trying."

She rolled her eyes again, already tucking it into her purse.

She liked the way he flirted—easy, low-pressure, like he wasn't trying to win a game, just enjoying the one being played.

They lingered over the last bites of dinner, not in a rush because the night felt like it was still unfolding.

Tariq pushed the last sushi roll toward her. "Go 'head. You know you want it."

"I'm full."

"You're lying," he said, dipping it in wasabi before offering it again. "Here. Last bite."

She took it with a smirk and popped it into her mouth. "You're annoying."

"You're welcome."

When the check came, Tariq slid his card into the folder without looking at it.

Jaqueline raised a brow. "It's like that?"

He leaned back, arms draped across the booth like it was a throne. "Look, if you wanna pay me for your Shirley Temple, I won't stop you. But yeah. I got it."

She smirked and sipped her drink. "I'm just sayin', most dudes at least pretend to argue about it."

"I'm not most dudes."

She leaned forward just slightly, chin resting in her palm. "So what kind are you?"

Tariq's smile dimmed into something smoother. "The kind that remembers what you wore the first time we met."

Jaq blinked. "What?"

"That lavender top. Off the shoulder. With your hair up and your hoops."

She reached for her clutch, half ready to change the subject and half ready to throw herself across the table. "So you just be out here with a photographic memory for women's outfits?"

"Only when the woman makes an impression."

Before she could fire back, the waiter returned, laying the check folder down with a smile.

"You're all set."

Tariq didn't open it right away. He kept his eyes on her. "So you gonna let me take you out again, or was this a one-time dinner with benefits?"

"Benefits?" she repeated, laughing.

"Yeah. Great company. That last bite. Me, absorbing your jokes and not taking offense."

She shook her head. "You're so full of yourself."

He grinned. "Maybe, but I'd rather be full of you."

Her mouth dropped open. "Tariq."

"Just sayin'."

She leaned back in her seat, fighting a real smile now. This man was dangerous, but in that good, warm way. Like a song you swore you wouldn't add to your playlist, but ended up on repeat anyway.

She folded her arms, eyes glinting. "We'll see."

"Bet," he said, grabbing the folder and slipping his receipt inside.

"C'mon," he said as he stood, offering his hand. "I want to show you something."

Jaqueline narrowed her eyes. "Isn't this how Dateline episodes start?"

He grinned. "I think you'd survive armed with those heels."

Jaqueline hesitated for just a beat, her hand hovering over his, then she smiled, letting her fingers brush.

Even as she stood, a tiny knot of doubt tugged at her chest. She knew the night was only beginning, and some things, some people, were never as simple as they seemed.

♪*Sugah Daddy* - D'Angelo and The Vanguard

14

The Girl Who Felt Watched

♪ *Crazy* - Gnarls Barkley

She hadn't planned to stop using it, but once she saw that strange symbol stitched into the lining, something in her said not to carry it anymore.

It wasn't just the bag. It was the dreams.

She never remembered the beginnings, only the middle. Her hands would be full. She'd be standing at a train crossing. Always alone. Always waiting. But no train ever came.

The first night she'd woken up sweating. The second, she woke up crying.

She hadn't told anyone. What would she even say? Hey, I think my Louis bag is giving me nightmares?

Her stomach had been queasy for days. She tried to shake the feeling by busying herself. She restyled her hair, put on music, reorganized her shelves, washed dishes. It helped a little, but she remembered something else.

The day Mrs. Bell gave her the bag she had leaned in close, adjusting the strap, and said, "Every young lady needs a bag that carries her forward."

Marie hadn't thought much of it then. She'd smiled, said thank you. But now, now it sounded like something else.

Marie pulled the bag from the closet. Inside, everything looked normal. No green glow. No creepy whisper.

Just a single strand of thread, knotted into a curl.

She didn't touch it.

She just stared.

And then, without knowing why, she whispered aloud, "You don't own me."

And zipped the bag shut.

By noon, Marie hadn't touched the bag again. It sat by the wall by the closet where she dropped it, like it knew it had no business being there. Like it was waiting on her to deal with it.

Instead, she lay across her bed with her phone on her stomach, ignoring the weird hum in her chest. Until her screen lit up.

B: My grandma asked if I was bringing "that girl." You rolling with me today?

Marie blinked, rereading it twice. Then a tiny smile crept across her face.

MARIE: "That girl" is wild. I still cant believe you told her about us.

B: You know she love you. She said she made that Mexican cornbread that only you two like

Marie rolled onto her side, thumb tapping the screen.

MARIE: What time you picking me up?

B: 3:30.

Marie smiled again.

B: You and my sister seem cool again. Got plans for another sleepover?

MARIE: The pool house idea was reckless. That's how we got caught remember?

B: Worth it but yeah we need a new location.

MARIE: Or a new situation.

B: You really tryna make me suffer all summer?

MARIE: I'm tryna make sure I survive summer.

B: Bet but if I was at your window right now you'd open it.

MARIE: If I had a dollar for every time you texted me "you up?"

B: That's an honorable text. It means I care about your rest.

MARIE: You care about my thighs.

B: Ok wow. I came to be loved not slandered.

MARIE: Boy that's your grandma's job

Things were easier when she was talking to him. Not because they'd solved anything, not because she'd forgotten that strange little symbol, or the feeling she couldn't shake. It was just that he made her laugh. He made her feel held, even when he wasn't touching her.

Marie got up, dragging herself to the mirror and swiped on a little gloss. She pulled out her outfit: a soft olive-green sundress that brushed her knees and a clean white pair of Air Force Ones.

Bryson pulled up right at 3:30, like he said. No honking, just the soft thud of his car door as he stepped out and made his way to hers like always.

His smile was wide and easy. "You look good," he said as soon as she opened her front door.

"You always say that," she mumbled as she locked up behind her.

"Cause you always do."

He opened the door for her and tossed his tablet from the passenger seat into the back. She slipped in, the car already cool from the A/C and smelling like citrus gum and his cologne.

He circled back around, slid into the driver's seat, and gave her a look. "So you not gonna tell me you missed me or nothing?"

She gave a light laugh, fingers fidgeting with her seat belt. "I just saw you like…days ago."

A few minutes into the drive, he reached over to turn the music down. "You okay?" he asked. "You been kinda quiet."

Marie hesitated. There it was again, his ability to see her even when she didn't want to be seen. She considered saying something, anything. But the truth felt too heavy.

"I'm fine," she said lightly, watching the trees blur past the window. "Just been in my head."

"About what?"

She turned to him, teasing. "You got time for a therapy session?"

He glanced over. "For you? Always."

The silence stretched.

Bryson eased them along the two-lane road, one hand steady on the wheel, the other drumming the beat of the song low on the stereo. A few minutes passed before he glanced at her again.

"Do me a favor?"

Marie looked up. "Yeah?"

"Text Grandma for me. Ask if she needs anything."

Marie picked up his phone from the cup holder and the screen lit up instantly.

The lock screen was a black background with a jagged crown drawn in thick strokes, three points tilted like it was ready to topple yet somehow holding steady. The Basquiat crown.

Of course, Bryson was claiming royalty without saying it out loud.

She swiped it open, thumb hovering. "You really gonna have me be your secretary?"

"Only person I trust," he said easily, eyes on the road.

Marie found Grandma's contact and typed:

Almost there. You need anything?

The reply came quick.

Ice.

Marie laughed. "She said ice. She still doesn't trust her freezer?"

Bryson shook his head. "I told her to get a new one. I might have to just pull up with it one of these days."

"Older people keep stuff until the wheels fall off." Marie teased

The gas station sign came into view against the late afternoon sky. Bryson flicked the blinker and pulled in.

Once parked, he killed the engine and leaned back. "You coming in?"

Marie shook her head. "I'll hold the fort."

He grinned, grabbing a crumpled twenty from the console.

"Cool. Sit tight."

She watched him stride inside easy and tall, shoulders rolling like he owned the whole world. Through the wide windows, she saw him heft a bag of ice from the cooler and then pay at the register.
When Bryson slid back behind the wheel, he asked, "You ever been to my grandma's without it being, like, a full family function?"

Marie shook her head. "No. Why? Is this a test?"

"Nah," he smirked. "You already passed."

He said it so matter-of-factually. Marie leaned back, still and soft and grateful.

They rode in silence for a bit, winding their way into the older part of town where houses had porches big enough for whole families.

Marie glanced around, picking at the gold chain around her neck, absently brushing her fingers along the curve of her name.

Up ahead, she saw the familiar hedges and the squat mailbox that leaned slightly to the left like it was trying to retire. A large oak tree reached over the front yard guarding the red brick home that never seemed to age.

Bryson slowed and turned into the gravel driveway, the crunch under the tires louder than expected. He killed the engine but didn't move to get out just yet.

Marie looked over at him, then at the front porch. A white rocking chair was swaying just slightly, though no one was in it.

Bryson rested his hands on the steering wheel, tapping twice before leaning back.
Marie glanced at him again. "What?"

He let out a low breath, almost a laugh. "You wanna know what she said? When I first told her about us?"

Marie tilted her head. "Yeah. What did she say? Don't lie to me either."

He grinned faintly, but it didn't reach his eyes. "At first I just told her I was seeing somebody. Didn't even say your name. Just... 'a girl.'"

Marie arched a brow. "That's all I got?"

He shot her a sideways look, guilty but playful.

"I couldn't leave it like that, so later that night, I called her back. Told her straight-up that it was you."

Marie's pulse picked up. "And?"

He turned to face her fully now, "She laughed."

Marie blinked. "She laughed?"

"Yeah," Bryson said. "Said, 'Baby, I already knew. You think an old woman don't see what's in front of her?'"

Marie's lips parted as Bryson reached for her hand across the console. "She said if I was man enough to call her back and say your name, then I was man enough to stand on it. That's all she wanted from me."

Marie's throat tightened. She squeezed his hand, then pulled it back gently, staring out the window again.

She pressed her palms to her thighs, steadying herself. "So what do we do now?"

Bryson smiled faintly. "We eat. Let her talk our ears off."

Marie exhaled, almost a laugh, but her chest still throbbed with something raw.

"Okay," she said softly.

"Ready?" he asked, glancing at her with that easy, confident smile.

Marie nodded, staying still as Bryson got out. She'd learned to allow him time to open her door— that first time she'd rode in his car to that soul-food spot far enough away that they wouldn't run into anyone they knew.

Bryson grabbed the ice from the back first, then opened the passenger door and reached for her hand. She let him lead her, gravel crunching softly underfoot.

"Feels like forever since we've just... been," he murmured before leaning down.

Their lips met. It was quick, soft, just enough to make her chest flutter.

When they pulled back, she laughed quietly.
"Come on," he said, flashing that teasing smile.

Hand in hand, they started toward the back of the house.

♪ *Lovin' You* - Minnie Riperton

15

The Girl Who Saw Through Smoke

♪ *I Can't Wait* - Sleepy Brown feat. Outkast

The grease was hot and ready. Mayfield stood on the porch behind her little brick house, apron tight around her waist, eyes behind sunglasses too big for her face but perfect for squinting at the sun. The fish, a clean batch of catfish seasoned the night before, sizzled the second it hit the pan.

"Sounds like it's talkin' to me," she said to herself, flipping one filet with a flick of her wrist.

A warm breeze carried the smell of jasmine from her garden. The vines had taken over her fence, curling like little hands around anything they could grab.

She stirred the cornmeal in the metal bowl, making sure it stayed fluffy.

She had a good view of the driveway from here. Wasn't nobody slick enough to sneak up on her. And today, she was expecting two of her favorites—one by blood, one by spirit.

She liked Marie.

That child had the kind of eyes that didn't judge you, but saw you deep down, past what you wore or how much money you had in your purse. And she was polite. Asked before taking seconds.

She looked out at her tomatoes, ripening just right. The okra had gone crazy this summer. Every time she turned around, there were more. She'd have to bag some up and send them home with Marie.

She heard a buzzing and reached over to grab her phone off the garden table. It was a text from Bryson:

Almost there. You need anything?

She texted back with one finger:

Ice.

She set the phone down and took a deep breath. Something in the air felt off. Not in a bad way. Just shifted.

All around her, the yard whispered. Even the bees were buzzing like they had something to say.

She wiped her hands on her apron and stepped back to admire the setup. Folding table dressed in a blue checkered cloth, and a pitcher of sweet tea.

The crunch of gravel snapped her head around as a familiar car pulled into the driveway. She could tell it was Bryson by the rhythm of the tires. Boy always drove too fast in the city, but slowed down when he hit her road like she'd trained him.

She smiled and wiped her hands again.

The car doors closed gently—one, then the other. No slams. Bryson knew not to bring tension onto her porch. Marie probably just knew it naturally.

She didn't rush to greet them. Let 'em walk up on their own.

Bryson came around the corner, tall and broad like his daddy.

Right beside him was Marie. She looked tired around the edges. Like someone who'd been holding her breath.

Grandma Mayfield smiled as she turned the fish one last time.

"Well, looky here," she said, not looking up. "Hope y'all hungry."

Bryson kissed her on the cheek and grabbed the bag of ice from under his arm. "Brought the ice."

"You brought a lot more than that," she said.

Marie stepped forward, a soft little "Hi, Miss Mayfield" on her lips.

Grandma turned, wrapping Marie in a hug. "There she is."

Marie smiled.

They sat under the awning in front of her big fan. Bryson filled cups with tea, Marie helped plate the fish, and Grandma kept an eye on both of them through her sunglasses.

Bryson kept watching Marie.

And Marie, she kept touching the strap of her dress like it itched.

Grandma leaned back and let the silence do the heavy lifting.

Then Marie spoke.

"Miss Mayfield do you believe in signs?"

The question floated like steam from a hot plate.

"I believe in the Lord. I believe He don't always use a megaphone."

Marie looked out toward the garden.

"There's been weird stuff lately," she said, hesitant. "Little stuff. Dreams."

Bryson shifted in his chair. He was watching Marie like he'd missed a page in the story.

Marie picked at her cornbread. "I thought it was just me until I found something inside my bag."

Mayfield's brow twitched.

Bryson looked over. "What do you mean?"

Marie hesitated. "Just a symbol tucked into the lining. Looked like somebody put it there on purpose."

Bryson looked confused. "Where did you get the bag?"

Marie paused briefly. "It's in the duffle your mom gave me for Christmas."

Bryson's face tightened. "So, what? You think my mom had it stitched with some kind of spell?"

"She ain't say all that," Grandma finally said, her tone level. "But you know your mama don't do anything without a reason."

She turned to Marie, "Sweetheart, sometimes people give you gifts with two hands, but one of 'em's holding something behind their back."

Marie nodded slowly, "I thought maybe I was overreacting."

Bryson's jaw clenched "What should she do? Like, should she just not wear it?" He asked.

"She can burn it," Grandma said, simple and plain. "Or bury it. Salt it. Cleanse it."

"But you don't be scared," she continued. "If there is somethin' stitched in there, it can't hurt you unless you let it. The Lord got bigger power than any stitchin' needle."

Mayfield saw the way Marie's fingers curled tighter around her napkin. The girl had been holding it together, but you could feel the edges fraying.

"I don't understand. Why would she do that?" Marie's voice cracked. "You think she knew there was something between us?"

Bryson blinked, as if trying to rewind some tape in his head.

As Marie's eyes welled up, Bryson moved closer beside her then pulled her into his arms.

"I swear to God, I didn't know she'd do something like that." He said, voice low and raw.

Bryson pulled back just enough to look her in the eyes.

"I'm not gonna let anything happen to you."

Marie didn't respond.

"Well," Mayfield finally spoke.

She didn't need to say more. The rest was already happening, whether they knew it or not. Some things didn't need fixing, just naming.

The rest of the meal passed in soft conversation and shared glances, the kind of quiet that follows truth like a shadow.

When it was time to go, they didn't announce it. They just moved in sync, clearing their plates, hugging and thanking Mayfield, moving as if the night had already told them everything they needed to know.

By the time Bryson's taillights disappeared around the corner, the sun had slipped low, and the porch lights flickered on.

Mayfield stood barefoot in the grass rubbing her hands together, slow. That girl was carrying more than just tension.

"Mmhm," she muttered to the night. "That child's pregnant."

She didn't need no test. It was her own dream that settled it. A baby in a river, floating peaceful on a quilt she didn't recognize. She'd woken up sweating, but calm. Now she understood why.

She'd seen it again tonight, plain as day. The faint flutter under Marie's jawline, that tiny, telltale pulse. Most wouldn't catch it. But Mayfield had been watching women for seventy-some years. She'd caught the same sign on her sister, on her own daughter, on the pastor's wife two weeks before that woman ever confessed. New life had rhythm.

Folks these days called it superstition, or chalked it up to coincidence. But Southern women knew. Their bodies were barometers, their dreams prophecy, and their instincts older than scripture.

In her day, getting pregnant young wasn't uncommon. It wasn't exactly encouraged, but it wasn't met with gasps either. Girls would miss a cycle, then miss another, and by the third they were out there with their bellies leading them. Nobody said congratulations. They just started sewing.

You married the boy, or you didn't. Sometimes you raised the baby yourself. Sometimes your mama claimed it as her "late-in-life blessing" and you pretended not to hear folks whispering behind their hands.

But it wasn't the pregnancy that brought shame. It was how people treated the girl who carried it. Like she'd swallowed sin whole. Like her body was a billboard for failure.

Mayfield had seen the weight of that shame bend women, had watched it fold strong girls down into something brittle. And now? These days it was different. Or it was supposed to be.

Now they said choice like it was freedom, like it was light. But the shame hadn't disappeared. It had just changed clothes. Became more sophisticated. It crept in through quiet judgments and people who swore they were supportive, just "worried."

If Marie was pregnant—and she was almost certain the girl was—then the question wasn't how it happened. It was what they'd do with the knowing. What kind of net the world would stretch under her.

She did have Bryson. And she had her.

And sometimes, that was more than most girls ever got.

Mayfield looked up at the sky. "Lord, let her be braver than I was."

She turned toward the house, her knees aching the way they always did after standing too long. The fireflies lit her path like lanterns from the other side.

She stepped onto the porch, careful not to track in grass, and closed the screen door behind her with a gentle slap.

Inside, the house had that after-company stillness, the kind where the walls seemed to settle back into themselves. Mayfield picked up a stray cup from the coffee table as she moved toward the kitchen. A pan still sat in the sink. She'd deal with that in the morning.

She set the cup down, then reached for the dish towel and wiped her hands. It was habit. The same way she'd hum to herself when her mind was working.

Mayfield pressed her lips together, then went to the sideboard and opened the drawer.

The small mason jar was still there, the one with the dried rosemary and lavender. She took it out, shook it lightly, and set it on the counter. Then she opened the second drawer, the one she didn't let folks go rummaging through, and took out a small bundle of twine and a packet of salt.

Mayfield tied the herbs with slow, practiced fingers, then set the bundle beside the jar. She wouldn't call it a protection charm, Marie might laugh it off or refuse it outright, but she'd find some gentler name. A "blessing bundle," maybe. Something that could pass as nothing more than a bit of old-lady fussing.

She turned off the kitchen light and started down the hallway. The air back here was cooler, the smell of clean laundry faint in the dark. She stopped at the hall closet, reached in, and pulled down a quilt.

It wasn't for her.

She laid it out on the couch in the front room. If Marie needed somewhere to breathe when she found out, somewhere that wasn't crowded with questions or judgment, Mayfield's house would be ready.

"Lord," she murmured, "keep that girl steady."

She went and sat on the porch, letting the night sounds carry her into the kind of thinking you only did alone, when nobody was around to hear you admit you were worried.

A soft shuffle at the gate made her glance up. Mr. Grove, the old man next door who had lost his wife last year, leaned on his cane, squinting toward her porch light.

"Evenin', Mayfield," he said, voice warm but hesitant. "Thought I'd stop by. I smell that fish you said you were fryin' for your grandson and his lady."

Mayfield's lips lifted. "You want some?"

He chuckled softly, shaking his head. "You know I can't resist."

She went to the kitchen, fixed him a plate, and handed it to him with a grin. "Careful, now."

He accepted it, and for a moment, they just stood there, the quiet of the yard wrapping around them. His eyes softened in a way that reminded her why she liked having him around, he'd been keeping pieces of her heart safe without her even asking.

"You been busy tonight," he said.

"Mmhm," she said, tucking a stray strand of hair behind her ear. "Having company makes a body feel young again."

He smiled, tipping his head. "I can see that."

Mayfield felt a warmth in her chest that had nothing to do with the hot air. For a few moments, the night held them in a quiet sort of promise, soft and safe, like a small secret tucked between neighbors.

"Go on home," she said, nudging him gently. "You'll spoil your appetite before you even take a bite."

He lingered just a second longer, looking at her like he wanted to say something more. Then, with a nod, he hobbled down the path, leaving her with the porch lights flickering above, the quiet night around her, and a smile she couldn't hide.

♪ *Killing Me Softly with His Song* — Roberta Flack

16

The Girl Who Wanted It All

♪*As* - Stevie Wonder

The dress came in a black garment bag with a gold zipper. Vanessa unzipped it slowly, holding her breath.

It looked like it belonged to someone who walked into a room and owned it. Someone who stood at the edge of a yacht with a champagne flute and everyone's attention.

Mrs. Bell had picked it out herself. Paid in full. No discussion.

"Think of it as an early welcome," she had said. "To everything that's coming."

Vanessa didn't ask what everything meant.

She stood in front of her mirror, pressing the dress against her torso. It shimmered, even in her bedroom's dull lighting. For a moment, it almost felt real. That all this plotting and waiting and well-timed smiles might finally land her where she belonged.

But even then, she couldn't help wondering if someone else was getting a dress too. Something cheaper. Something that didn't need a zipper because it could be slipped on.

She hated how Marie lived at the edge of her thoughts now.

Her mom knocked lightly on the door before coming in.

"You're gonna wrinkle it pressing like that," she said, eyeing the gown. "Is this for his birthday party?"

Vanessa nodded, still looking in the mirror.

"You sure you wanna let her play stylist too?" her mother asked, testing the waters.

"She knows what looks good on me. And I'm not about to tell her no over a dress." Vanessa answered.

"Just make sure you're doing it because you want to, not because you think you have to."

Vanessa smiled, "I am."

Her mother paused, like she was holding space for something unspoken.

"Okay," she said, with a quiet breath. "Just checking."

The moment passed, light on the surface but heavy underneath. Vanessa didn't say much after that, but that night, she couldn't sleep.

She tried scrolling but it made things worse, so she gave up and pulled out the photo box tucked in the back of her closet.

She flipped through until she found the one of her at seven years old, standing on the sidewalk in front of their house, arms crossed in an glittery pink coat. Behind her, across the street, Bryson was mid-air on a skateboard. Blurry, but unmistakable.

He'd always lived just close enough to be around, far enough to stay a mystery.

Their parents were neighbors who turned into friends. That meant backyard brunches together in the summer and Christmas parties in the winter, the kind of gatherings where the adults laughed too loud and drank too much while the kids got sent off to "bond."

His mother would nudge him toward her, and hers would do the same, both pretending it was innocent.

When she was thirteen, she remembered sitting on her front steps watching the sunset when he crossed the street and handed her a red freeze pop like a peace offering.

"It's still hot out here," he'd said, grinning.

It was nothing, but she'd still replayed it for weeks.

They went to different high schools. She was at St. Mary's, a private school, and he went to Oak Hill. One time his school beat hers at homecoming and he'd said, "Y'all tried," with that lazy, teasing confidence that got under her skin.

Nothing deep. But after that, he always waved when she came outside, sometimes with that same smirk.

Vanessa had the dress.

She had the blessing.

She had his mother already on her side.

So why couldn't she sleep?

Bryson had looked good at brunch, too good, honestly. Like someone who didn't know he was being watched, or worse, someone who did and just didn't care.

She slid her pinky under her bonnet, scratched her temple, and rolled over onto her back.

She opened her texts, scrolled to Amani and typed:

You up? I have to update you on the whole Bryson situation.

She stared at it a beat. Then followed up.

His mom threw this fancy brunch and guess who wasn't there?
Seconds later, her phone buzzed.

AMANI: *That little artsy girl?*

VANESSA: *Ding. Ding. But it's crazy. It still felt like she was there.*

AMANI: *What does that even mean?*

Vanessa hesitated. Then typed.

VANESSA: *Idk he just wasn't himself. Looking around like he lost something.*

AMANI: *I cant believe you still feeling him like that.*

VANESSA: *Idk what I'm feeling. Maybe it's just that I used to be the one folks expected him to like.*

AMANI: *So what are you going to do?*

Vanessa bit her lip.

VANESSA: *I got this gorgeous dress his mom bought me. I'll make sure he sees what he'll be sleeping on.*

AMANI: *Okay petty princess. Just don't play yourself in the process.*

Vanessa tossed the phone down.

She wondered what would happen when Marie showed up. What Bryson would do. What she would do.

She picked up her phone again, thumb hovering before she scrolled to Cash Bennett's name. Tall, nice body, nice smile. Cash was easy. Always ready to respond.

VANESSA: Random question. You still think about me?

It took less than a minute for his response.

CASH: Hell yeah. More than I should.

She smiled at the screen, leaning back.

VANESSA: I was just making sure. Would hate to think I fell off your list.

CASH: Nah you are the list.

Her laugh was quiet but real. She could practically hear his voice saying it, all cocky but earnest.

VANESSA: Flattery's a cheap trick.
VANESSA: I like cheap tricks.

CASH: I've got a million of them. You free tonight?

She let that sit for a second, tapping the screen like she was thinking about it.

VANESSA: Maybe but I've been told I'm dangerous when I'm bored.

CASH: So be bored with me.

VANESSA: Tempting but I don't take requests.

CASH: Then make it a surprise.

VANESSA: You couldn't handle that kind of surprise.

CASH: Try me.

She stretched her legs out on the bed, staring at his last message. She could keep this going, let him spin up some fantasy in his head, maybe even agree to see him. But that wasn't the point. The point was the reminder, for both of them, that she could make someone chase her without even leaving the house.

Vanessa typed.

Maybe I will.

She deleted it. Instead, she locked her phone, leaving his last message unanswered. She would let him think about it. Let him check his phone every few minutes.

At some point she must have dozed off, because she woke with her bonnet halfway off and her arm numb from falling asleep on her phone.

Her garment bag still hung from the closet door, gold zipper catching the first rays of light.

She rolled over, groaning, grabbed her phone, and squinted at the screen. There were five unread messages.

They were from Cash.

Her stomach tightened. She hadn't expected him to actually say much more. Usually he kept things light, feeding her lines until she either humored him or left him on read. This was different.

CASH: I don't know what you're doing but whatever game this is I'm not playing.

Her thumb hovered above the screen. She swallowed, sat up straighter, and scrolled.

CASH: You hit me out the blue like you get bored and spin the wheel, see who picks up.

Vanessa blinked hard, suddenly wide awake. He wasn't finished.

CASH: Always needing the attention but never wanting the person. It's not cute. It's sad.

She sucked her teeth but couldn't look away.

CASH: Don't get it twisted. I wanted you. Still do to be honest. But you don't text me for weeks and then come around when your ego needs food? Nah.

The final message landed like a slap.

CASH: Go figure yourself out. I'm done.

Her chest burned. She stared at the phone until the screen dimmed and went black.

She threw it to the other side of the bed, yanked her bonnet off, and pushed both hands through her hair.

"Boy, please," she muttered to no one. But her voice cracked, just slightly.

She swung her legs over the edge of the bed and sat there, bare feet pressed into the carpet. Her room felt smaller than usual, like all the air had been pulled out of it.

She wasn't supposed to feel this way. Not over Cash. He was a side character.

Still, she felt it. That tiny sting of rejection, the fact that he had closed the door first, not her.

Vanessa got up and paced, arms crossed. She told herself it didn't matter. She had bigger things in play. A whole future she'd been angling toward.

Her phone buzzed again, and she snapped her head toward it, pulse spiking. It wasn't Cash, just a group chat notification.

Vanessa dropped the phone face down on the sheets again.

For a second, she wished she could text Amani about it, get one of her sharp but comforting replies. But she already knew what Amani would say.

She picked up her phone again, deleted the unread notification banner, and shoved the whole thing under her pillow like it couldn't haunt her there.

Vanessa sighed and headed for the door, telling herself to focus. The kitchen might offer some clarity, or at least caffeine.

She slipped down the stairs, the morning light slanting through the windows, painting stripes across the floor. The smell of toast and coffee hit her as she rounded the corner, then she froze.

Her father sat at the table, a grapefruit sliced perfectly in half in front of him. He held a spoon in one hand, a folder of travel documents propped against the coffee cup in the other. Bags lined the doorway, stacked and zipped, ready to be wheeled out to the car.

"Morning," he said, his voice low but sharp.

Vanessa forced a polite smile and crossed her arms. "Morning."

He tilted his head, studying her the way he always did, like he could see through her skin. She had learned over the years that look was the precursor to a lecture.

"Coffee?" he asked, gesturing to the counter.

She shook her head. "No, thanks." Her stomach twisted.

He stabbed a spoon into the grapefruit, careful, precise, then leaned back in his chair. "You look… awake."

Vanessa ignored the comment. She leaned against the counter, watching him like she hadn't seen him in years, even though he'd been in the house. He chewed slowly, then reached for a napkin.

"You've been reckless," he said casually.

"Excuse me?" Vanessa asked, raising an eyebrow.

"Your credit card," he clarified, voice calm but firm. "I saw the statements. This isn't just a little splurge here and there, Vanessa. This is excessive."

Vanessa pressed her lips together, resisting the urge to roll her eyes. "It's my money. I pay it back."

"Do you?" he asked, leaning forward slightly, spoon paused mid-air. "You may think a designer dress or a dinner out won't matter, but they add up. Sooner or later, the credit card company doesn't care how charming or beautiful you are, and neither will the kind of husband you say you want. No man worth his salt wants a wife who spends his money before he can even make it."

She crossed her arms tighter. "I'm responsible," she said, the words clipped, like she was trying to convince the both of them.

He shook his head, the mild disbelief clear on his face. "Not enough. You've got to be strategic." he said flatly. "Money is power and you're wasting yours chasing fleeting satisfaction."

Vanessa pretended to be focused on the grapefruit, but she couldn't. She felt the familiar mix of frustration and unease tighten in her chest.

She hated lectures, especially when they landed with truth she couldn't deny.

He leaned back, folding his hands over the folder of travel documents. "Look, I know your mother and I have been… guiding you in a way. But you need to start guiding yourself too. You're smart, capable, and frankly, you've got potential. Don't blow it on impulse purchases because it makes you feel bigger or more important than you really are."

She wanted to snap back, defend herself, but the words wouldn't come. They were lodged somewhere between stubbornness and truth.

Her father set down the grapefruit, wiping his fingers. "I'm headed for Chicago today," he said, nodding toward the bags lined up by the door. "I'll be gone a few days. But while I'm gone, I want you to think about what I said."

Vanessa nodded, feeling the weight of his gaze. "I will."

"Good." He stood and headed for the door.

She exhaled, shoulders stiff, watching him leave, the door clicking softly behind him. The grapefruit sat half-eaten, still glistening with juice. She stared at it, thinking about the neat, ordered life everyone wanted her to have—the life her father, Mrs. Bell, and society had laid out like a perfect spreadsheet.

She thought of the dress, hanging silently in the closet. She thought about the sting of Cash's words, sharp and unavoidable: **It's not cute. It's sad.**

She headed back upstairs and retrieved her phone from under the pillow.

She typed:

I get it. I really do.

She hesitated before hitting send, her finger trembling. Then she pressed it, watching the message disappear into the void.

Seconds stretched. She tapped her phone again, almost impatiently. And then it buzzed.

CASH: Good. That's a start. But don't think this fixes anything. I'm done with the games. You're smart, Vanessa. You know better. Act like it.

♪ *Roses* - Outkast

17

The Girl Who Counted

♪ *Throw It In The Bag Remix* - Fabolous feat. The Dream

She got a formal invite for Bryson's birthday party. An embossed envelope tucked inside her mailbox like something from a wedding planner instead of Mrs. Bell.

Jaqueline grinned "You better come correct. Heels, hair, real-deal glam."

Marie nodded like she had it all together. Like her stomach wasn't rebelling over the green smoothie she'd tried to finish that morning.

They were shopping in the fancy part of town. Jaq held up a satin dress in champagne gold and raised her brows. "Be honest, too much thigh?"

Marie shrugged, trying to keep the edge out of her smile. "Not enough."

Jaqueline grinned, tossing it over her arm. "You know I like to give just enough to start a rumor."

They moved through the racks. Marie couldn't find anything that didn't feel tight or itchy.

"You good?" Jaqueline asked, pausing with a sequined halter against her chest. "You been real quiet."

Marie forced a small smile and tugged at the hem of a flowy white wrap dress. "Yeah, just tired. My mom's been making me drive her around here and there."

Jaqueline was still riding her own high.

"I forgot to tell you how the date went," she said, suddenly glowing.

"After sushi, we went for a drive. He said he wanted to show me something."

Marie raised an eyebrow, waiting.

"He took me to this overlook. He was playing D'Angelo. It was giving grown and intentional."

Marie laughed.

"After that, we went back to his place. I didn't even mean to stay that long, but… whew."

"I'm confirming the rumors," Jaqueline said, fanning herself. "I'm talking playlist right, lighting right, he even had fresh roses on the counter like he knew I was coming."

Marie grinned, shaking her head. She was glad her friend was happy. Tariq had seemed like the real deal from jump.

They moved to the accessories. Marie held a pair of gold earrings up to her ears, then put them back down. She needed to buy a gift too. Something for Bryson that didn't feel loaded or emotional or like it was saying more than it should.

Maybe cologne.

Her stomach clenched.

"You okay?" Jaqueline was watching her again. "You look like you saw a price tag with a comma."

Marie swallowed. "Just hot. These lights."

"Wanna sit down?"

"Nah, I'm good."

Jaqueline moved on, talking about heels and whether she should wear her hair up or down.

Marie followed her voice, nodding at the right parts. But inside, everything felt shaky.

By the time she got home, she was done pretending. The bag with Bryson's gift sat unopened on her desk. The dress she picked for herself hung on the back of her door. Her bra was somewhere on the floor, kicked off as soon as she walked in.

She sat cross-legged on the bed with her calendar app open. Counting.

Backwards.

Twice.

And then again.

That was… five weeks ago?

Her mouth felt dry. Her chest tight.

Marie closed the app and leaned back on her bed. She stared up at the ceiling like it could help her solve this.

She hadn't taken a test. The idea of standing in a checkout line with that box in her hand made her want to disappear into dust.

Still, she needed to talk to someone.

Her thumb hovered over Jaq's name in her messages. No.

Mom? Definitely not yet.

Then she scrolled to Bryson.

She tapped the call button before her brain could talk her out of it.

One ring. Two.

"Yo."

She blinked hard. "Hey."

"Hey, you good?"

"No." It fell out before she could catch it.

The silence on his end tightened. "What's up? Where you at?"

"At home. I—" She rubbed her forehead. "I just... I'm not feeling right."

He sounded instantly alert. "You need me to bring you something?"

She hesitated. "I just... I think I might need to get a test."

Another pause. And then his voice. "What kind of test?"

She didn't answer.

After a second, he exhaled. "Okay. I'm about to come get you."

When she finally heard him pull into the driveway, Marie stepped outside and locked the front door behind her. The screen door eased shut with that soft hiss and click.

Bryson didn't say anything at first. Just watched her for a second, then walked around and opened the passenger door like it was second nature.

She slid into the seat without a word.

Bryson rounded the car, got in, and adjusted the AC. "You ate anything today?"

Marie gave a half-shrug. "I couldn't."

"I know a drugstore out the way," he offered. "Kinda ratchet, but quiet."

"That's cool," Marie said softly.

They rode with the speakers low.

They'd been driving for a while, far enough that the landscape changed a little. The gas stations weren't the ones she recognized anymore.

The drugstore had faded signage and a parking lot full of cracked lines. Bryson pulled into a space near the entrance and killed the engine.

"I'll go in with you," he said, reaching for the door handle.

Inside, the fluorescent lights made everything too bright. Marie kept her sunglasses on as they walked toward the pharmacy section, past aisles of discounted seasonal candy and clearance.

The pregnancy tests were behind a locked glass case.

"Of course they are," Marie muttered.

A teen employee wandered over. "Y'all need something?"

Bryson pointed. "Yeah. That two-pack at the top."

The kid raised his eyebrows just slightly, then went to find the manager with the key.

Marie leaned into him. "I hate this."

"I know."

"I feel like everybody's staring."

"They're not."

The manager arrived and unlocked the case without comment and handed Marie the test. When they got to checkout, Bryson gently took it from her hands and placed it on the counter with a bottle of water and some gum.

"I got it," he said without looking at her.

The cashier rang them up like it was allergy meds. Just another transaction.

When they got back to the car, Bryson opened the door for her again

"Thanks," she said as she settled in.

Bryson nodded. "We'll figure it out."

He pulled back onto the road.

They still had to find somewhere to take the test.

Marie sat quiet, elbow pressed to the window, watching the rows of dollar stores and tire shops blur past. The bag with the test sat by her feet, crackling every time the car hit a bump, like it wanted to remind her it was still there.

Bryson's hand rested on the steering wheel, calm. He hadn't said much just checked on her with glances that lasted longer than required.

Then he said, "There?"

Marie blinked. "Where?"

He nodded ahead. "Big Bean."

It was a squat little coffee shop with string lights on the windows. It looked clean and empty enough.

"Yeah," Marie confirmed.

Before she could even reach for the door handle, he was already getting out to open her door.

She stepped out slowly, adjusting the strap on her purse where the test was shoved deep.

"I'm right here. Text if you need me."

Inside, the air was thick with espresso and burnt cinnamon. She kept her head down and found the bathroom tucked behind a bookshelf full of mugs.

Her hands were already on the box before she knew what she was doing. Her fingers trembled as she unwrapped the packaging.

She sat on the lid, balancing the test across her knee, and whispered a prayer.

When it was done, she placed the test face-down on the edge of the sink and stood with her back to it. Eyes closed.

The bell above the coffee shop door rang when she stepped back into the parking lot. Bryson looked up immediately.

She didn't say anything, so his eyes scanned her face like he was checking for damage.

He opened the door for her and she got in, but didn't buckle her seat belt right away. She just sat.

He got in too, but he didn't start the car.

"You okay?" he asked, voice soft.

She didn't answer.

She just reached into her purse, pulled out the test, and held it out to him.

Bryson stared at it. Then at her.

"No doubt about it, huh?"

She shook her head.

"Well shit."

Marie didn't look at him.

"We grown. It's not like we 16. We'll figure it out." He trailed off.

Marie flinched at the word "we," like it was too easy, too soft around the edges. Like it didn't touch the parts of this that scared her most.

Bryson looked down at his wrist, thumb brushing the edge of the watch face like it could slow everything down.

"You don't get it," Marie whispered. Her voice wasn't sharp, just tired.

Bryson turned toward her, but he didn't speak.

"I'd be the one on campus with a belly," she said, eyes locked on the windshield like she couldn't afford to look at him.

"I'm the one who'd have to leave class to throw up."

Bryson opened his mouth. "Okay, but..."

"You won't be the one that professors assume isn't serious anymore, or the one that everybody thinks messed up."

The words came faster now, like they'd been bubbling just beneath the surface.

"I'm the first in my family to even go to college."

She could still hear her mother's voice echoing in the back of her head: "You need to be thinking long-term, Marie."

"You act like I wouldn't be there." he said, frustration in his voice.

Marie exhaled. "Right, you'd get to be the golden boy with a baby on the way. Meanwhile, I'd be the girl who threw away her scholarship for a boy who never even claimed her in public."

Bryson's jaw tightened.

"That's not fair," he muttered.

A long silence fell.

Bryson started the car.

"You already made up your mind, haven't you?" he asked.

"Bryson, I'm scared."

"I am too," he admitted.

She looked over at him for the first time since she got in the car.

"But I'm not gonna let you sit here and act like I'd just disappear if you had it."

She swallowed hard.

"I didn't say you'd disappear. I said...I'm not ready."

"Neither am I," he said, "But shit, Marie. That don't mean we can't do it. You act like we can't do this."

He reached across the center console and touched her hand.

"Look. I'm not gonna force anything," he said. "Whatever you decide, I'm in your corner. But don't shut me out."

Marie didn't answer.

Bryson leaned back into his seat.

"I got you," he added softly. "Even if you don't believe it."

The car was silent for a while except for the buzz of the engine and the rhythm of her heartbeat in her ears.

"When do you think it... happened?" he asked, like he didn't know if he should.

After that first time, the space between them kept shrinking. Every touch was familiar now, practiced and eager.

They were still careful, always protected, until that one time.

"That night we watched Love Jones, we didn't have anything, and you said..."

"Don't do that," he interrupted. "Don't put this all on me."

"I'm just saying," she said. "You told me...and I didn't stop it either, so."

Bryson ran a hand down his face.

"Damn," he muttered. "This is wild."

"We were being reckless," she said.

"Yeah," he agreed. "But I don't regret being with you."

There was a pause.

Bryson didn't push her to say more. Just shifted the car into drive and pulled out of the lot like he already knew where he was going next.

Five minutes later, they pulled up to a drive-thru near the bypass.

"Tell me what you want," he said.

"Fries and a strawberry shake," she answered.

He glanced over. "That's it?"

A few minutes later, he handed her a strawberry shake and a greasy bag with a chicken sandwich, fries, and an a slice of pie. She smiled. He always did too much.

They drove on, paper bags and shakes between them. By the time they reached the beach, it was mostly empty except for a couple taking photos by the dunes.

Bryson killed the engine and looked at her.

"Wanna get out?"

Marie hesitated, then nodded. "Yeah. I think I do."

They walked in slow steps shoes in hand, salt clinging to the air, the breeze carrying away the pieces of the day they weren't ready to face.

Marie didn't say much, but her mind was loud.

Every step tugged her closer to a thought she'd been dodging since she saw the test, the art show.

Her work made the cut. Her professor had called it "emotionally layered." Said it moved people. That it spoke.

Now, she couldn't stop thinking about how she could be showing up to her first art show with a secret pressing up against her ribs. Another heartbeat.

The waves hissed.

Beside her, Bryson walked close enough that their arms bumped every now and then.

She wondered if he'd come to the show. If she'd still feel like an artist by then, or just someone who used to be one.

Marie tilted her head back and stared at the stars, wishing one would fall just for her. She didn't need answers, just a sign.

The sky didn't move.

Maybe tomorrow she'd start figuring it out.

Tonight, she just needed the water and the feeling that the world hadn't stopped spinning yet.

Bryson glanced at her, eyes soft. "You good?"

Marie paused. "No."

♪ *Slummer* - Killer Mike feat. Jagged Edge

18

The Girl Who Had Enough

♪*Devil in a New Dress* - Kanye West feat. Rick Ross

The yacht was nothing short of stunning, exactly what she expected of her mother. It was crisp white with brass detailing, floating like a glass of champagne on the marina. Velvet ropes and candlelight, florals on every table, even a soft jazz trio playing when Jaqueline first stepped onto the deck in heels she absolutely did not need, but wore anyway because the aesthetic demanded it.

The dress code had been "summer formal," which really meant "southern money" in practice. The guests were draped in linens and lace, silks and sculpted curls. Jaqueline's bronze dress hugged her like it had been sewn on and her hair slicked back into a bun that could cut glass. She'd pulled up with Marie, of course, who looked stunning in ivory.

Marie wasn't talking much, but her eyes darted everywhere. It wasn't long before she spotted Vanessa, standing near the bow with a flute and a smile that didn't touch her eyes. The gown she wore shimmered when she moved.

Vanessa kept glancing toward the entrance, and sure enough, Bryson arrived with a small crew of guys from school. His energy shifted when he spotted Marie, and Jaq caught it even from across the deck.

Marie tried to play cool, tried to focus on the charcuterie table like she cared about fig jam. But Jaqueline watched her friend's shoulder tense, like the whole yacht had tilted under her heels.

Girl, just breathe.

Mrs. Bell floated through like the yacht was hers. She smiled at guests with that subtle jaw-clenched pleasantness she'd mastered over years of networking and manipulation.

When her eyes met her mother's, something passed between them. Her mother gave her a tight nod and moved on.

As the sun dipped lower the lights on the yacht glowed golden. The DJ played *"Curious"* by Midnight Star and couples started dancing. That's when it happened.

Bryson walked over and held out his hand to Marie.

She hesitated. Just for a second. Then took it.

The two of them moved into the center of the yacht's deck, and was too late to hide. People were watching.

And her mother saw.

Jaq wasn't sure what she expected, maybe a dramatic scene. But no. Her mother just stood there, lips pinched, nodding along to the music with eerie calm.

Jaqueline saw Bryson lean close to Marie. She couldn't hear what he said, but Marie's laugh floated back toward her like a memory. She was happy with him, and they didn't even have to say it.

Tariq appeared by Jaqueline's side with a glass of something sparkling and fruity. "You see them?" he asked, nodding toward the pair.

She sipped. "Hard to miss."

"You still mad?"

Jaqueline raised a brow. "I've graduated past mad."

Mrs. Bell drifted toward Jaqueline.

"Lovely night," she said, glancing around. "Everything is beautiful and going to plan, as usual."

Jaqueline narrowed her eyes. "I'm sure it is."

Mrs. Bell's smile didn't crack. "Vanessa looks radiant in that dress, doesn't she?" Delilah said lightly. "Almost like it was made for this moment."

Jaqueline's stomach dropped.

"And Marie?" Mrs. Bell added, tilting her head. "Well. She always had an interesting energy. I just hope she knows what she's doing."

It wasn't what she said. It was how she said it.

Jaqueline didn't raise her voice. Didn't toss her drink or call her mother out in front of everyone.

Jaqueline just smiled, let out a breath, and walked off.

Then the splash came.

Gasps rose in a wave. A glass shattered against the deck.

Jaqueline's eyes darted fast looking everywhere for Marie.

She pushed to the railing, heart hammering, eyes scanning the water, then the crowd, then back again.

She didn't see Marie. Was it Marie?

That ivory dress. She remembered helping zip her into it hours earlier, remembered the soft fabric, the delicate stitching near the back.

Now, all she could think about was that dress soaking, ruined, clinging to Marie's skin while people pointed and whispered.

But it wasn't her. The crew was pulling up some guy in an Armani suit.

Jaqueline stepped back trying to get her pulse under control.

Her hand landed on her chest.

It wasn't Marie.

Thank God.

Tariq found her on the lower deck five minutes later, holding a napkin full of strawberries

"Was it you?" she asked, raising an eyebrow. "Did you push somebody in the water? Be honest."

"I'm innocent," he said. "But I thought about it when the DJ started playing *Return of the Mack.*"

She didn't laugh, not really. Her body was still humming with adrenaline.

Tariq stepped closer, his tone shifting. "You okay?"

She let out a breath. "Yeah. Just...that reminded me how fast everything can change."

She didn't mean to sound that dramatic, but she was tired of pretending everything was fine. The party was gorgeous and expensive in all the right places, but her nerves had been frayed since Marie sat down at her vanity hours earlier and whispered, "I'm pregnant."

That moment was still spinning around her skull.

At first, Jaqueline didn't say anything. Just stared at her best friend, sitting there with her lips pressed together like the secret might shatter her from the inside.

"I don't know what I'm gonna do," she said quietly. "So don't tell anyone. Not yet."

Jaqueline nodded before wrapping her arms around Marie and holding on tighter than she meant to.

Then she whispered the only truth she had.

"You can still have it all."

She had meant it, but now, here on this yacht with her mother, Jaq wondered if it was actually true. All she knew was, the closer the truth got to the surface, the more dangerous the water started to feel, and someone had already fallen in.

The lower deck had gone quiet. The music from above thumped like a muffled heartbeat, and for a moment, Jaqueline let herself enjoy the distance.

It was the only place on the yacht where she didn't have to smile or pretend to be flattered by compliments laced with comparison. Tariq was at her side, one arm stretched behind her along the cushions, his fingers idly grazing her shoulder.

Then came the click of heels.

"Wow," Vanessa said, stepping down with a sigh, her voice coated in something between amusement and annoyance. "Y'all hiding down here?" Vanessa asked.

Jaqueline gave a dry smirk. "Not hiding. Recovering."

Tariq gave a polite nod. "Evening."

Vanessa barely looked at him, eyes already returning to Jaqueline. "You look nice," she said. "Is that the dress from that boutique on Edgewood?"

"Yeah." Jaqueline smoothed her hand down the fabric, unbothered. "You've got a good eye."

"I try," Vanessa said. Her tone was friendly on the surface, but there was something else underneath. She looked around the lower deck, like she was waiting for someone to appear. Her smile twitched slightly.

"You know, I always admired how Marie let you shine. She's got such a low key energy. Not the kind of girl who needs the spotlight."

Jaqueline blinked. "That's because she doesn't have anything to prove."

"Mmm," Vanessa said. "That must be nice."

Tariq cleared his throat and shifted slightly.

Vanessa smiled at both of them, then added, "Well, I should get back upstairs. Your mom wanted a picture before the cake comes out. You know how she is about capturing the moments."

She turned, heels clicking again as she made her way toward the stairs.

213

But just before she disappeared, she paused at the bottom step and looked back.

"Y'all coming?"

Jaqueline stared at her, then leaned her head against Tariq's shoulder. "Nah. We're good."

Vanessa's smile didn't falter. She just nodded once and kept climbing.

When she was gone, the silence snapped back like a rubber band.

Tariq exhaled. "Damn. She's…"

"Something," Jaq finished for him.

The boat shifted slightly beneath them, soft creaks in the wood and the hum of bass from upstairs wrapping around the quiet.

"She said she misses when we were friends," Jaqueline added.

Tariq let the sentence settle. "Do you believe her?"

Jaqueline sighed. "Part of me wants to. But I also know Vanessa doesn't say things unless she wants something."

He nodded. "Even when she's soft with it, it's still strategy."

"That's the scary part." Jaqueline pulled back enough to look at him. "You start questioning everything. Even the good memories."

Tariq's gaze didn't leave hers. "That ain't your job."

She blinked. "What?"

He shrugged, casual but steady. "To figure out everybody's motives. Sometimes it's just about watching what they do when they think no one's watching."

She tilted her head. "Since when you sound like somebody's therapist?"

"I moonlight," he said with a grin.

She curled her legs underneath her and leaned into him again.

"Thanks," she said quietly.

"For what?"

"For not making me explain everything."

Tariq smiled, but didn't look smug. "I got patience. Especially for you."

"I think she's gonna stir something," Jaqueline said finally, voice low.

"Then let her stir it," he said.

Jaqueline gave a dry laugh and reached for his hand. Their fingers laced together easy, like they'd done it before in some other life.

Her bronze dress was gleaming, even in the low light.

"You know you killing 'em tonight, right?" he said, voice low, smooth enough to melt.

She arched a brow. "Killing who?"

"Everybody upstairs. Whole yacht." His gaze traveled slow over her, just appreciating. "But me the most."

Her laugh was soft, almost disbelieving. "You always talking slick."

"It's true." He said, leaning a little closer.

Her pulse skipped. She tried to mask it, but the way he looked at her made it impossible.

Then he kissed her.

The gold of his grill was cool against her lip, sharp where everything else was heat.

When his hand slipped to her waist, drawing her toward him, she didn't resist. His fingers trailed lower, resting on her thigh, then brushing the hem of her dress.

"Tariq" she said softly, pulling back a fraction.

He stilled immediately, eyes locked on hers. "You want me to stop?" His voice was calm, like stopping wouldn't undo him.

She shook her head, breath catching. "It's not that. Just… someone else could walk down."

His grin was slow, teeth flashing. "Let 'em. You think I care? I finally got you right here."

Her stomach fluttered. "Got me, huh?"

"Yeah." He slid his hand up, palm spreading over her hip, tugging her closer. "But the question is… do I got you for real?"

"What are you saying?"

"I'm saying, officially. Will you be my girl?"

She blinked, stunned at how easily he'd said it.

"Yes, no, maybe," he added with a teasing tone.

She smacked his chest lightly. "You really giving me a 'maybe' option?"

"Of course," he teased, voice light again. "Gotta give you room to overthink it, right?"

She laughed, head shaking. But when she looked at his eyes, the laughter faded into something softer, something that scared her a little.

"Yeah," she said. "I'll be your girl."

He exhaled, slow and satisfied, like she'd just confirmed what he already knew. Then his grin spread, dangerous and boyish all at once. "Say it again."

217

She narrowed her eyes, but her smile gave her away. "I'll be your girl."

That was all it took.

His lips traveled from her lips, to her jaw, to her throat, to the delicate skin just under her ear. His breath was hot, words murmured between kisses.

"You don't even know what you do to me."

Her nails grazed his neck as his lips brushed hers again, slow and lingering. "I'm not hiding you. Ever."

Her heart pounded. She should've been nervous, but instead, she felt steady.

She was his.

♪ *Take Away* — Missy Elliot feat. Ginuwine

19

The Girl Who Held On

♪ *You Send Me* - Sam Cooke

It happened fast, but in her memory it stretched long, like film unspooling in slow motion. One shove, clean and deliberate, then the man's body arced backward, his eyes flashing more with surprise than fear.

A crew member vaulted from the deck, voice commanding. They caught the man's thrashing arms and dragged him toward the ladder, hauling him up slick with seawater.

"He's fine!" someone called, voice high and trembling.

The slap of the wind off the water felt sharper after it happened, like the air itself had opinions. Behind her the music still played, like nothing had gone wrong.

She stood at the far edge of the upper deck, both hands gripping the polished railing.

Bryson hadn't said a word since.

He was a few feet away, pacing like the deck couldn't hold him still. The muscles in his jaw jumped every time someone glanced over. Marie had seen him angry before, but never like that. Never reactive.

It hadn't even looked real when it happened. One second, the guy had muttered something slick under his breath, something about her, and the next, Bryson had planted a single hand on his chest and sent him over the side.

"Bryson," she said softly, afraid to break the night even more. "What were you thinking?"

He turned to her, eyes unsettled. "He said your name."

Marie swallowed. "That's not enough reason."

His voice lowered. "It is to me."

She looked out over the water again, trying to slow her breathing.

Jaqueline had warned her earlier that evening. "If you feel tired, or off, or overwhelmed—you don't owe this night anything."

But Marie wanted to be here. She'd wanted to feel normal, to wear the dress, to pretend that her body wasn't changing and her future wasn't tightening around her.

She heard footsteps and turned to see Bryson standing beside her again.

"I'm sorry," he said.

Marie didn't answer right away. She didn't have anything sharp to say, no moral to hand him like a punishment. She was just tired.

She turned to him, finally meeting his eyes.

"You pushed somebody off a boat," she said flatly.

"I'd do it again," he said, just as flat.

She hated how part of her wanted to laugh, and how another part wanted to lean into him so hard she'd disappear.

Then came the heels as Mrs. Bell glided toward them.

She looked immaculate, as always. She was in silk in cream tones that somehow stayed pristine despite the open sea air. She wore a single strand of pearls, and that smile that said "don't cause a scene" louder than words ever could.

"Marie," she said, voice like fine china. "Bryson."

Bryson stiffened beside her.

Marie swallowed, the taste of iron rising behind her throat.

Mrs. Bell's eyes moved back to her. "You look tired."

Marie resisted the urge to touch her face, to smooth her dress. "It's been a long day."

"I imagine," she said turning to Bryson. "Though some of us seemed to find interesting ways to break the monotony."

His jaw locked.

Mrs. Bell's voice remained calm. "I'd rather not embarrass anyone with a conversation about liability. But since we are floating, I'd ask you both to remember that accidents have a way of drawing attention."

She stepped closer, just enough to drop her voice into something only Marie and Bryson could hear.

"There are people on this boat who are watching you. People who make decisions that last longer than one impulsive evening. So if you care about your future, if either of you do, I suggest you remember how easily impressions stick."

Marie's stomach twisted.

Bryson opened his mouth, but Mrs. Bell cut him off with a look.

"Don't make it more than it already is," she said.

Then, as if summoned, she smiled brightly and turned to float back across the deck, stopping just long enough to compliment someone's shoes.

Marie couldn't breathe for a moment.

"Are you okay?" Bryson asked.

She didn't answer. Just stared at the place where Mrs. Bell had been, her whole body burning with something between humiliation and rage.

Marie didn't think, she just moved.

She was halfway across the deck, already weaving her way through laughter and clinking glasses.

She crossed the floor in silence, steady, each step lighter than the one before it.

She caught up with Mrs. Bell near the dessert table, where someone was raving about creme brûlée.

Mrs. Bell turned at the sound of her name, expecting flattery, not fire.

Marie stood in front of her, calm and clear-eyed. "Can I speak with you?"

Mrs. Bell blinked, smile twitching. "Of course, darling." She gestured politely toward the far end of the deck.

They stopped near the rail.

"I know what you're doing."

Mrs. Bell tilted her head. "You'll have to be more specific."

Marie's voice didn't shake. "The bag. Whatever that was supposed to do."

Her eyes narrowed.

"You want me to disappear. You want me to shrink, to apologize. But I'm not sorry and I'm not going anywhere."

Mrs. Bell folded her arms, that smile still playing at the corners of her mouth like it had nowhere else to go. "You're very brave."

Marie scoffed. "I'm not brave. I'm tired."

Mrs. Bell's face shifted, barely, but it was enough.

Marie gave a quiet nod, like she'd confirmed something for herself.

"Have a lovely evening," she said softly, and walked away.

Marie didn't know where she was going exactly. Her feet carried her down the narrow staircase to the lower deck. The lighting shifted the further she went, like the party was shedding layers the deeper you walked.

She got to the bottom of the stairs and froze.

Jaqueline was there, pressed against Tariq.

Jaq must've felt the air change, because she pulled back and Tariq straightened instantly, wiping his hand over his mouth like that could erase what Marie just saw.

Jaqueline blinked, her expression snapping from caught to composed in a breath. "Hey," she said, too casual.

Marie's throat went dry. "Hey," she managed

Jaq sat up straighter. "You okay?"

Marie didn't answer right away. Just exhaled slowly and leaned her back against the wall opposite them.

"I talked to her," she said finally.

"Who? My mom?" Jaqueline asked.

Marie nodded.

Jaqueline's brows lifted. "Are we talking 'polite confrontation' or 'knuck-if-you-buck' type energy."

"I just told her the truth, that I know what she's doing, that I know she had that symbol put in my bag, and that I'm not afraid of her."

Jaqueline stood and crossed over to her, wrapping her in a hug. "You didn't have to do that alone."

Tariq stood, brushing off imaginary lint from his jacket. "I would've paid to see her face."

They all laughed soft and exhausted, then the door creaked open again.

This time it was Bryson, shoulders squared like always. He paused, taking in Jaq, then Tariq, then Marie.

"Birthday boy," Jaqueline said with a grin.

Bryson gave a slow nod. "I was wondering where y'all went."

Tariq glanced between Bryson and Marie, then offered a hand. "We haven't met yet, have we?"

Bryson stepped forward, gripped it firm. "Nah. But I heard about you."

Tariq smirked. "Hope it was the charming version."

Bryson raised a brow as they all laughed.

Jaqueline nudged Marie's shoulder. "You going back up?"

She nodded. "Yeah. I am."

They took the steps back up to the main deck, Bryson with his hand resting easy at the small of Marie's back and Jaqueline on Tariq's arm.

Tariq talked the DJ into playing the real electric slide, Marcia Griffith's "Electric Boogie."

The yacht had found its rhythm again and everyone with good knees was on the dance floor.

Then someone dimmed the lights, the music dipped into the background, and a few people started to gather near the cake table.

Someone shouted, "We need the Birthday boy!"

Bryson groaned, trying to play it cool, but Jaq pushed him toward the crowd where the candles were already flickering.

The cake was almost too perfect to eat. It was three tall tiers covered in flawless white fondant, smooth as porcelain. A thin navy ribbon edged each layer and the top was crowned with delicate gold sugar orchids. The whole thing sat on a marble stand like a museum piece.

Marie couldn't help but smirk. Bryson had said he didn't want anything big.

Mrs. Bell stood off to the side, watching it all unfold. Her expression was unreadable, like she'd swallowed the lemon in her champagne. She didn't move to join the singing, but everyone else did, off-key, loud, and full of messy joy.

"Haaaaappy biiiirthdaaay to yooouuuu…"

Bryson pretended to be embarrassed, but Marie saw that little lift in his chin. He liked being seen.

When they reached the last line, he locked eyes with her. Just for a second. Long enough for the air to shift.

"Haaaaappy birthdaaaay, dear Bryyyyyson…"

Marie sang it soft. But it felt like her whole chest was in it.

He blew out the candles in one breath and claps erupted like it was a concert.

"Speech!" someone yelled.

He waved them off, but then looked toward Marie again. "I'm just grateful," he said, casual and low. "Grateful to be alive, to have y'all here, and to be... surrounded by real ones. Yeah, I might've baptized dude tonight, but in my defense, he was asking for it."

A relieved laughter broke out across the deck.

"Also, let the record show I had a full plate in my hand. So really, I was the victim."

More laughter. Someone clapped.

"But anyway, thank y'all for pulling up. For real."

He lifted his glass slightly, eyes catching Marie's again.

"To good people, and good decisions."

Cheers rang out, a few people tapping glasses. Someone shouted, "Too late for that last part!" and he just grinned.

Mrs. Bell approached as the DJ eased the music back in. She placed a hand on Bryson's shoulder. "Lovely speech," she said with a tight smile.

And then she turned and walked right past Marie without a word.

Marie got a slice of cake and made her way over to where Vanessa was standing alone by the railing. She approached slowly. She didn't even mean to approach at all. Her body just moved, like some unseen tide had nudged her there.

Vanessa's dress shimmered faintly in the light and looked impossibly delicate now, like it had started to fray.

Marie didn't say anything. She just leaned beside her, watching the water catch the moonlight.

"You look nice," Vanessa said after a pause.

"So do you," Marie replied.

"You should be careful," Marie said quietly. "You're standing kinda close to the edge."

Vanessa didn't flinch. "It's not that far of a drop."

There was a long silence. Just water and wind.

Finally, Vanessa turned just enough for Marie to see her profile.

"I used to think you were my competition," she said suddenly. "But you weren't. Not really."

Marie raised a brow, caught off guard by the confession. For a moment, she considered brushing it off, letting the silence close in again. But there was something fragile in Vanessa's voice, like glass about to splinter.

"You know," Marie said softly, "sometimes we spend so much time thinking about what we're chasing, we forget that maybe there's something better waiting for us."

Vanessa gave a short, humorless laugh. "Sounds easy when you say it."

"It's not easy," Marie admitted. "But you're... you. You're a force." She gave a small shrug. "The universe doesn't waste people like you."

Vanessa blinked at her, lips parting just slightly. Then she looked away, out toward the horizon where the water stretched endless and silver.

Then she walked away, moving like someone who had just laid something heavy down.

Marie turned and walked back toward the dance floor, feeling the tug of her dress against the wind, the heat of gazes.

Jaqueline was pulling people onto the dance floor and demanding the DJ cue up "Before I Let Go," because it was still a Black party no matter how many hors d'oeuvres there were.

Bryson slid in behind Marie just enough to let her know he was there.

"You okay?" he asked under the music.

"I will be," she said, breathless but certain.

He nodded, then leaned down just enough to whisper in her ear. "You're glowing."

Marie rolled her eyes.

When the song ended, someone shouted for a group photo. They packed together near the bow laughing. Marie found herself between

Jaqueline and Bryson. Jaqueline squeezed her hand and the flash popped, capturing the moment forever.

As the party settled back into the harbor, Marie wandered below deck for a breath. She found her reflection in the mirror above the bar and barely recognized herself. Not because she looked different, but because she felt different.

Her fingers brushed the necklace at her collarbone, and something in her steadied.

Then her gaze dropped. Past her chest, all the way to the gentle slope of her belly beneath her dress. She pressed her palm there. Although nothing showed, the weight of what was inside her pressed against her heart. Fear crept in again, sliding cold fingers up her spine. Could she do this? Could she carry a life and still carry herself?

The smile she'd worn upstairs faltered, trembling in the glass.

Behind her, a voice said softly, "Ready to head out?"

She jumped, wiping her hand against her side as if she could erase the gesture. Bryson stood leaning against the door-frame, jacket in hand. His eyes caught the worry etched across her face.

"Marie." He said her name like it was fragile, like it might shatter if he was too loud. He stepped closer, lowering his voice. "I know you probably have to head home soon, but maybe we could just… find somewhere quiet. Talk more. Just me and you."

Her throat tightened. "Bryson…"

He shook his head, closing the space between them until he was just a breath away. "I don't care that it's my birthday. I don't care about the party. I care about you. And I can see it, you're still scared. You don't have to hide that from me."

Her hand trembled as she finally let it fall back to her belly. "I just... I can't stop thinking about what our parents would say if they knew."

Bryson covered her hand with his, warm and solid, like an anchor.

Marie exhaled shakily as he brushed a tear from her cheek with his thumb, "C'mon. Let's go."

♪ *Try Me*- James Brown

20

The Girl Who Lost Her Grip

♪*U Used 2 Love Me* - Rapsody

Delilah Bell had always believed in preparation.

Some women floated through life, waiting for things to happen, but not her. She built her future brick by brick, planned the angles, and polished the details.

In a world that loved to see women like her fall, Delilah stood tall because she knew the game and refused to play it sloppy.

Which was why she had a plan for Bryson before he ever left diapers.

The boy was golden from birth. He'd always had sharp eyes, a steady smile, and charm that didn't need training. She knew he'd go far if she kept the road clear and she knew exactly who belonged at the end of that road, Vanessa.

Vanessa with the fine-boned face and pedigree smile. Vanessa with parents who sat on boards and made calls that moved money like her and her husband.

She placed the idea in Bryson's ear since he was old enough to understand. Gentle nudges at first, then stronger— Vanessa would look good on his arm, Vanessa's family understood their circles, Vanessa was the kind of woman who made men into kings.

Delilah had paved the road so carefully. And yet, here they were.

The Bell house was quiet that afternoon, the kind of quiet Delilah never trusted. Bryson's footsteps came heavy down the hall. She set her magazine aside, already bracing.

He entered the living room with that set jaw she didn't like.

"Ma," he said.

"Baby," she answered, smoothing her blouse. "You sound tight in the chest. What's wrong?"

"We need to talk."

Her heart pricked, but she smiled anyway. "Well, that sounds serious."

"It is." He said, still standing.

Delilah sat back and crossing her legs, bracelets chiming. "Go on then."

Bryson dragged a hand across his jaw. His eyes were blazing.

"I need you to hear me all the way through," he said. "No cutting me off."

That tone, it wasn't her boy's tone. It was a man's.

Delilah folded her hands, gave a nod. "I'm listening."

"You've had this whole thing mapped out for me since I was a kid," Bryson started, voice tight. "Who I'm supposed to be, what I'm supposed to do, who I'm supposed to marry. You made it clear Vanessa was the one."

Delilah didn't flinch. "And she is. Vanessa's perfect. You could do a whole lot worse."

He let out a sharp laugh. "That's the problem, Ma. You never even asked me what I wanted. You just decided."

Delilah's jaw ticked. "I decided because I know what it takes in this world. You think I worked this hard just so you could throw it away on—"

"On Marie?" His eyes cut into her.

Delilah kept her face still, though her chest clenched. "So you're finally gonna say it out loud."

Bryson stepped closer. "You've been pushing Vanessa down my throat since middle school. I thought if you knew about Marie, you'd ruin it. And come to find out, you already tried. Behind my back."

Delilah felt heat crawl up her neck. "Watch your tone."

For a second she saw the boy she raised again— fire in his eyes, stubborn as stone.
"Marie told me everything. You tried to get rid of her like she was nothing?"

Delilah's throat went dry. That girl. That bold little thing had stood on the yacht and dared to face her.

"She's not nothing," Delilah said carefully, words tasting bitter. "But she's not Vanessa. One day you'll thank me for trying to keep you on the right path."

Bryson's laugh came harsh. "The right path? Or your path? Because the way I see it, you don't care what makes me happy."

The accusation sliced, but Delilah swallowed it down. Smile. Always smile.

She leaned back, crossing her arms. "That girl's already got you tied up in knots."

Bryson's jaw flexed, then he said it, flat and certain.

"She's pregnant."

Delilah's smile slipped.

"What?"

His voice didn't waver. "Marie's pregnant. We're pregnant."

The room spun, her breath hitched, but she forced herself steady.

"Well," she said, voice sharp as glass, "isn't that just like y'all. Already making reckless choices. You're twenty years old, Bryson. Twenty. And you're bringing a baby into this? Lord have mercy." Her nostrils flared. "I gave you every advantage, and you do this? Throw it away for some girl with no name, no money—"

"That's all you care about." Bryson snapped. "Money and status. You think love doesn't matter because it never mattered to you."

Delilah felt the sting but kept her chin high. "Love doesn't pay bills. Love doesn't open doors."

"I don't need your doors." He leaned in, voice low but burning. "And you keep dangling money like it makes you queen of this family. I've been making my own investments *and* I have my own place."

Delilah's heart slammed in her chest.

"You want to play grown man, then don't come crawling when it gets hard. Don't come asking me for help."

Bryson's eyes didn't move. "I'm telling you, if you wanna be in my child's life, you're gonna have to let go. No more trying to control me. No more Vanessa dreams. No more plans you made without me."

The words stung, sharp enough to draw blood.

She breathed once, then tilted her head, "Bryson... do you even hear yourself? A child having a child. Do you honestly think that girl is ready? Do you think you're ready?"

"I'm ready enough," he said firmly.

She gave a humorless laugh. "Ready enough to ruin your future." She leaned forward, searching his face. "Baby, listen to me. You don't have to do this. Nobody would blame you for making a different choice. Nobody would even have to know."

He blinked at her, disbelief and fire mixing in his stare. "You want me to tell Marie to get rid of our baby? It that what this is?"

Delilah swallowed, throat dry. She forced her tone light again. "I'm saying you deserve options. That's all."

Bryson shook his head. "You already have Marie doubting herself. You know why? Because on top of everything else, she knows what you tried. Who wants to have a child with someone who's mother tried what you did with that bag? I'm trying to convince her that we can fight through it. That we're stronger than what you tried to do."

Delilah's chest burned.

"And you know what makes it worse?" His voice rose, eyes narrowing. "You know Marie. You've known her since seventh grade, Ma. She's been in this house more times than I can count. How could you not like her? How could you look at someone who stayed up all night with Jaq when she got dumped, who brought you flowers that one Mother's Day when Jaq forgot, and act like she's nothing?"

238

Delilah flinched.

"She volunteers at the art center, she checks on her grandma every week. She's sweet, she's smart, and you want me to believe she's not good enough for me? No, Ma. This can't be about her. This must be about you."

Delilah's jaw clenched. For a moment she thought she could outlast the fire in his voice. But something inside her cracked.

"Oh... so do you think this is just about you?" she snapped, her silk composure tearing at the seams. "Do you have any idea how much me and your father carried to keep this family where it is?" Her voice rose, sharper, fuller. "The Bells and the Morgans together. Do you know what that would've meant? Two empires merging. Your children would have never had to wonder where they belonged, because they would've had everything, Bryson!"

The words slipped out before she could catch them.

Bryson froze, staring at her like she was a stranger.

"I'm thinking about our name," she whispered. "Our legacy."

Bryson's laugh was bitter, broken. "I am your legacy, and I'm telling you, if you haven't already messed everything up, Marie is going to be part of it too. Whether you like it or not."

The room seemed to shrink around them.

"I love you, Ma," Bryson said, softer now but no less steady. "But don't get it twisted, I have no problem loving you from a distance if you keep coming for her. If you keep coming for us."

Delilah wanted to scream. She wanted to shake him until he remembered who raised him. She wanted to slam the table, call that girl every name she had lined on her tongue.

She sat back, smoothed her blouse, and smiled, even though her chest felt like it was caving in.

"Well," she said lightly, "sounds like you've got it all figured out."

Bryson didn't smile. He just held her gaze for a long moment, then turned and walked out.

The door shut behind him and the house went still again.

Delilah sat frozen, her smile slipping the moment he was gone. She rose slowly, climbed the stairs, and caught her reflection in the landing mirror.

Her son was gone, her plan was in shreds, her control slipping like sand through her fingers.

She thought of Vanessa. She thought of Marie. And then she thought of a baby.

Her first grandchild.

The idea cut both ways, terror and sweetness all at once. She hated it, the way her hands already itched to hold a baby.

She pressed her palms flat against the cool edge of the hall table, steadying herself. The word "baby" refused to loosen its grip on her chest.

When was the last time she'd even held one? She had to go back years, maybe to her sorority sister's grandson, a soft bundle who smelled of milk and lavender. Babies had a way of searing themselves into memory with their warmth, their helplessness, their scent.

This was not the child she had imagined, not the one she had planned. For years she'd allowed herself the quiet indulgence of picturing what Bryson and Vanessa's children might look like: Vanessa's narrow nose, light eyes, and refined curls. The kind of children who belonged on the covers of alumni magazines and investment brochures. A continuation of the Bell story told exactly the way she wanted it read.

But today, against her will, her mind betrayed her. It started sketching new possibilities—Marie's wide brown eyes, Bryson's smile that cut both sweet and dangerous. Maybe a little girl with dimples. Maybe a boy with a head full of curls.

Delilah closed her eyes hard. "No," she whispered to herself. Not that. Not her.

Bryson had made it seem like Marie wasn't sure if she wanted to keep the child. That detail had snagged her, thorn-sharp. She wondered if she could still fix it. She had money and she had the connections. She could offer Marie more than she'd ever dreamed of. If it was a question of support, Delilah could supply that in abundance.

The image slid into her mind, uninvited, sitting Marie down across the table, speaking gently, making an offer. "You don't have to do this the hard way. If you want to attend a prestigious art school, I'll pay for it. If you want freedom, I can make that happen."

It could work. She could steer this whole thing back toward safety.

But the second Bryson found out, he'd never forgive her. He'd do exactly what he said, love her from a distance, keep her at arm's length, and she'd lose him for good.

That was the bind. That was the catch.

Delilah sank into the nearest chair, silk blouse whispering against the fabric. Her head tipped back, eyes closed, heart pounding against her ribs. She hated the choice in front of her. Step in and risk her son's love, or stay out and risk watching her legacy unravel in someone else's hands.

She had spent her life avoiding chaos. And here it was, in her own house, wearing her son's voice.

Preparation. Planning. Control. These were the tools that had always saved her. They could save her now too.

♪ *I've Been Loving You Too Long*- Otis Redding

21

The Girl Who Stayed Still

♪ *Father I Stretch My Hands* — Pastor T.L. Barrett and the Youth for Christ Choir

Renae woke with the kind of heaviness that only prayer could lift. She sat at the edge of her bed, hands clasped, whispering her usual thanks before slipping in a few petitions— for strength, for clarity.

In the kitchen, gospel music drifted from the radio while she whisked eggs, humming along between verses. The smell of butter and salt filled the house, spilling into the hallway where sunlight touched the family photos lining the wall.

Every few minutes, she paused to listen for movement from Marie's room. Nothing.

She plated breakfast for Marie anyway and left it covered on the stove before heading back to her room to dress. She stood in front of the mirror, smoothing the front of her church dress, and tried not to think too hard about how quiet the house felt when Marie was home but somewhere else entirely.

By the time she fastened her earrings and found her purse, the breakfast was still untouched.

She sighed, then walked down the hall and knocked lightly on Marie's bedroom door. "Marie? Are you going to church this morning?"

"Yeah," came her daughter's muffled voice from inside.

Renae hesitated a moment before pushing the door open. Marie was sitting on the edge of her bed, slipping on her ballerina flats. There was something about the way she held herself that made Renae's chest tighten. She had known, even before she knocked, that something had gone wrong at the yacht party. Marie wasn't usually like this, not after a night of celebration.

"Baby, I'll drive if you want," Renae offered, keeping her voice gentle.

"No, I'll drive," Marie said. Her eyes didn't meet her mother's.

Renae nodded silently. She watched as Marie slung her bag over her shoulder and stepped out the door, the faint scent of her perfume trailing behind her. There was a stiffness in her movements, a caution Renae hadn't seen before. She felt the pulse of worry tighten in her chest but reminded herself to let her daughter lead this morning.

Inside the church, Renae took a deep breath, letting the familiar scent of polished wood and flowers wash over her. She greeted people on the way to their pew, hugging, smiling, asking about children and grandchildren. Marie followed, offering polite smiles but nothing more.

When they sat down, Marie smoothed her skirt and stared straight ahead, hands folded tightly in her lap. The choir began to sing, voices rising like waves. Renae tried to lose herself in the sound, alto steady, hand swaying just slightly. Marie kept still.

When the pastor took the pulpit, Marie shifted in her seat, like she was bracing for something.

He smiled faintly, adjusting his mic. "Now, I wasn't gonna start with this story today," he began, "but something in my spirit said maybe somebody needs it."

The congregation murmured in agreement.

"I'll never forget the first time I tried to teach my son to ride a bike," he said, a grin tugging at his lips. "I thought, 'This is simple. How hard can it be?' Well, it turns out, very hard."

Pockets of laughter erupted.

"He fell, more times than I can count. I was frustrated, I was tired, I was ready to give up. But every time he got back on that bike, I realized something… God was in the teaching, not just the riding."

He paused, letting the message settle over the congregation.

"And isn't that how children are? They test us, they challenge us, they push us past what we think we can handle. Children are assignments.

God doesn't give us what we can already do…He gives us what will stretch us, grow us, and reveal His patience in us."

The congregation erupted in "Amen."

Renae felt the familiar ache of understanding twist in her chest. She glanced at Marie and noticed the tremor of tears that she quickly blinked away.

Midway through the service, Renae realized Marie was gone. Her heart thumped with anxiety. Maybe she'd gone to the restroom, she reasoned, or maybe she needed a moment alone. The thought of something more serious made her stomach tighten.

Renae waited almost twenty minutes, eyes constantly scanning the doors, the aisles. When she finally stepped outside, she spotted Marie sitting alone in the Tahoe, relief and worry colliding in her chest.

"Baby, are you okay?" Renae asked softly as she opened the door.

"I had a headache," Marie murmured, her voice faint. "Probably from all the perfumes." She gave a small shrug, trying to make it sound casual, but Renae could see the tension in her shoulders, the tightness around her eyes.

Renae reached across and touched her daughter's hand. "You scared me, baby. I was worried something had happened."

Marie shook her head, managing a small, distracted smile. "I'm okay. Just needed some air. Some quiet."

Renae nodded, and climbed in the passenger seat beside her daughter. She stole a quiet glance at her daughter's profile, the way the sunlight caught her hair, the small rise and fall of her chest with each breath.

As they drove home, Renae's mind drifted back to a memory she hadn't thought about in years. Marie had been in middle school, terrified of a school play where she had to recite lines in front of the entire auditorium. She had begged to stay home, to skip the performance, claiming she was sick.

"Baby," she had said, "I know you're scared. But you're stronger than you think. I'll be right here the whole time."

Marie had still gone on stage, hands trembling, voice shaking, but she had made it through. Renae remembered the pride swelling in her chest as she watched her daughter, radiant even in her fear. Even then, she had carried too much, but she had done it anyway.

Now, years later, Renae realized that nothing had changed. Marie still carried the weight of the world with her, still braced herself against storms. She still feared judgment, feared making mistakes, feared losing control. But just like that night in middle school, she would survive. She would find a way forward.

Back home, Marie disappeared into her room without a word. Renae assumed she needed space, but less than an hour later, the door opened again.

Marie stepped out, a touch of lip gloss, her hair smoothed like she had somewhere important to be.

"I'll be back for dinner," she said, slipping her phone into her bag.

Renae studied her for a moment, the careful polish of her outfit, the flicker of nerves behind her composure.

After tidying the breakfast dishes and straightening the kitchen, Renae did what she did every Sunday, she picked up her phone and called her cousin Yvonne.

"Hey, girl," Yvonne answered on the third ring, her voice warm, tired but cheerful. "How's everybody doing?"

Renae smiled, despite the knot of worry twisting her stomach. "Marie seems...good. Mostly. Doesn't really talk much. Just went quiet, stays in her room."

There was a pause on the other end. "Hm. That's Marie for you."

Renae exhaled softly. "Yeah. And there's that boy. I think there's something going on between them. I've suspected it for a while, but she never brings him up, never brings him over. She's so secretive about it. I just, I don't know how to handle it. I want to help, but I don't want to push."

Yvonne's voice softened, thoughtful. "Renae, listen to me. You already know Marie loves you. You just have to stay present. That boy, well, he's a piece of the puzzle, but he's not the whole picture. She just needs to know that she's seen and supported, no matter what."

Renae nodded, even though Yvonne couldn't see her. "I just want her to lean on me."

"She'll come to you when she's ready." Yvonne said. "You keep being that steady presence. That's all she needs right now."

Renae felt the tension in her chest ease slightly. "Yeah. You're right. I can't fix everything, but I can be here."

"Exactly," Yvonne replied. "And don't forget, Marie's more capable than she even realizes."

Renae smiled, a slow, grounding smile that carried years of hope and worry. "Thank you, Yvonne. I needed that."

"Anytime," Yvonne said.

After ending the call Renae moved into the kitchen with the quiet focus of habit. She pulled out the roasting pan, unwrapped the brisket, and began trimming it down with long, steady strokes. A rub made of brown sugar, paprika, and cayenne waited in a bowl nearby.

Her phone buzzed against the counter. She wiped her hands on the dish towel and checked the screen.

MARIE: Is it okay if I bring a friend to dinner?

Renae's knife paused mid-trim. She read the message twice, lips pressing together before she called out, "Babe, can you come here a second?"

Her husband stepped in, smelling faintly of cedar. "What's going on?"

She held up the phone so he could see. "Your daughter wants to bring a 'friend' to dinner."

He let out a low chuckle. "Guess I better make sure this brisket comes out right then." He went over to the sink to wash his hands. "You know I like handling the meat anyway."

Renae shook her head.

The rest of the afternoon slipped into its slow rhythm. The house filled with the warm, peppery smell of meat in the oven. Renae moved between side dishes, whisking vinaigrette for the salad, peeling potatoes. They fell into their old dance, moving around each other with quiet efficiency, the radio low in the background, sunlight shifting across the counters as the hours stretched.

Renae looked out the window and said, "They're parking now."

Her husband didn't respond right away. He was checking the brisket in the oven like it was a science experiment. Renae heard him close the door gently, and wash his hands without a word. She'd told him to act normal, but they both knew what that really meant, try not to say the first thing that comes to mind.

She smoothed her blouse with one hand and reached for the tray of cornbread with the other. Everything was ready. The food. The house.

She heard the car door close.

Renae moved to the front door, opening it before Marie and Bryson had even made it to the porch. Marie blinked, surprised. Bryson gave a quick smile.

"Hey, Ma."

"Hey, " Renae said stepping aside to let them in. "Come on in, food's hot."

Her husband met them with a nod and a half-hug for Bryson. "How's your people?"

"Good, sir," Bryson said, polite as ever.

They sat at the table, plates filled, glasses refilled, and still nothing was said.

Renae let it stretch.

Marie picked at her food, and Bryson kept glancing her way like he wanted to reach under the table and hold her hand but didn't know if now was the right time.

Finally, Marie set her fork down.

"There's something we wanted to tell y'all," she said.

Renae folded her napkin, slow and deliberate. "We're listening."

Marie looked at Bryson. He nodded.

"I'm pregnant," she said.

Renae didn't flinch. She just let it land in her chest like it already had a place there. Her husband cleared his throat, but didn't speak.

"Alright," Renae said, nodding once. "Okay."

Bryson shifted forward in his seat. "I know this isn't what anybody expected, but I'm here. I want to be here. I'll take care of whatever she needs."

Renae looked at him for a long moment. Then back at her daughter.

"You scared?" she asked gently.

Marie hesitated. "Yeah."

"Good," Renae said, and finally smiled. "That means you understand what's coming."

There was a pause.

"You think I'm disappointed?" she asked.

Marie's eyes welled. "I don't know."

Renae reached across the table and placed her hand over her daughter's.

"I'm a little worried," Renae said. "But not disappointed. "You're just... early."

That made Marie laugh through her tears. "Early?"

"You know what I mean," Renae said, squeezing her hand. "You're going to be fine. Both of you. All three of you, if you let people love you right."

She turned to Bryson, her tone a little firmer. "And you're not just here to say the right things, are you?"

She noticed the watch gleaming at his wrist. Not flashy, just timeless. The kind of thing a boy inherited from a man who taught him how to show up.

"No, ma'am," he said. "I'm here because I love her."

Renae, for the first time in weeks, felt peace settle back into her bones.

From the other end of the table, her husband cleared his throat.

Renae looked over, giving him the space to speak.

He set his fork down with the kind of care that always meant he'd been thinking longer than anyone realized. He looked at Bryson first, then Marie.

"I remember when your mother first told me she was pregnant," he said.

Marie's eyes widened slightly, caught off guard.

He nodded. "Didn't tell nobody at first. I was scared. Didn't have no plan. Just a pair of work boots and a used truck with no air conditioning."

Renae smiled faintly, but didn't interrupt.

"The thing I got right?" He said. "I stayed, even when I didn't know what I was doing."

He looked Bryson straight in the eye.

"Now I ain't saying y'all are us. You're not. You've got more options. More knowledge. But don't think for a second that love alone is gonna carry this. Love's the engine. But the work. That's the fuel."

Bryson nodded. "Yes, sir."

"And if you say you love my daughter," he continued, "you better love her in public, in private, when she's tired, when she's strong. You don't get to pick and choose."

"I understand," Bryson said, and this time his voice didn't shake.

Her father leaned back in his chair, picked up his glass of tea, and took a sip like nothing more needed to be said.

Renae gave Marie's hand one last squeeze, then let it go.

"Now," she said, "y'all want to tell the rest of the family, or should we?"

Marie smiled. "We'll tell them."

After dinner, Marie and Bryson lingered on the porch swing, talking low, sharing something Renae couldn't quite hear through the screen door. She let them have that. Let the night fall around them like a soft quilt.

Inside, she moved through the house in that familiar way all women move in their own kitchens. She rinsed the last plate, dried her hands, and turned down the stove even though it was already off.

The house had quieted, but not gone still. You could feel the pulse of it, of life being made, reshaped, passed down.

She walked down the hall, past the framed photos lining the wall— Marie with missing teeth, Marie as a baby being held by her father, Marie's high school graduation photo.

There was a kind of ache in watching your daughter become a mother. Not because you didn't think she could do it, but because you knew what it would cost her. The quiet sacrifices no one ever applauds.

Renae made her way to the living room and turned on the old stereo by the window. It took a minute to warm up, it was one of those CD changers that still had gospel stacked between Bob Marley and The Isley Brothers.

She flipped through the binder and found what she was looking for.

She remembered the first time she heard it. Marie had played it on the drive to Atlanta, windows down, both of them tired and sun-drunk.

She pressed play. The opening chords drifted through the house raw and slow, like molasses.

She sat back on the couch, letting the music curl around her. Her husband passed through, paused at the door-frame, then came to sit beside her without a word.

Marie would be alright. She wasn't fragile. She was forged. Through family, through faith, through the heat, through Sunday dresses, and every time she thought she'd break but didn't.

Outside, the porch swing creaked gently as Marie and Bryson's laughter rose.

Renae smiled, then she let the tears come. Not from fear or grief. Just from the sheer, unshakable truth of loving something you can't hold still.

♪ *Gimme All Your Love* - Alabama Shakes

22

The Girl Who Broke the Pattern

♪ *Don't Let Me Be Misunderstood* — Nina Simone

Sunlight slipped through the tall windows of the dining room, catching on the silver picture frames that lined the buffet. Family portraits, frozen smiles. Her wedding photo with the man she'd been paired with, chosen for her, not by her. A younger version of herself with eyes too bright, a smile too fixed. And Vanessa, year after year, bow tied around her waist, hair slicked into place, perfect even then.

The coffee on the table had gone lukewarm by the time her daughter finally wandered in. Vanessa didn't greet her, just lowered herself into the chair.

Her plate sat in front of her untouched.

"You should eat," Serena said gently, the words more plea than instruction.

Vanessa shrugged. "Not hungry."

She stared down at the table, not at the food. Her fingers tapped once, then she curled them into her lap.

Serena's chest ached at the sight. Because she knew that slump, that hollowness. She had carried it herself once. And she knew, just as surely as she knew her own name, that something had broken inside her daughter last night.

It reminded her too much of herself.

Prom night, 1984. Satin gown, pale pink, chosen by her mother. It had been stitched by the family seamstress, though not just with thread. Later, she would recognize the tiny, hidden pattern, the knots at the seams.

Serena hadn't understood it then. She only knew that when she stepped out of her room, her father's face glowed with pride. "Just wait until the Morgan boy sees her," he had said, his voice heavy with expectation.

She had gone to that dance not as a girl, but as a prize. She could still feel the stiffness in her shoulders as she posed for pictures, could still taste the metallic tang of nerves on her tongue as the Morgan boy shook her hand. His eyes had roved over her like she was an asset already signed over.

Later, she would marry him. Not because she loved him, but because it fit. Because it was expected.

He was handsome enough. Not cruel, not unkind. Just deliberate. His smile never stretched too far. His hands always rested heavy on the table, knuckles squared as though holding down something invisible.

On their wedding night, she lay beside him, staring at the ceiling beams of the hotel suite, and told herself this was what security felt like. Solid. Predictable. She pressed her hand over her own racing heart, urging it to slow.

Years passed, measured in holiday dinners and bank statements. Her role was clear: keep the house immaculate, keep Vanessa polished, keep herself unscandalized. She learned how to smile for pictures without ever showing too much. She learned which questions to never ask her husband, and which answers to supply before he even asked.

Still, sometimes in the quiet, after the lights dimmed and everyone was asleep, she felt a small tremor in her chest. Not regret, exactly. More like... ache. A wondering of what it would've been like to marry for something wild, something unruly, something like love.

Her stomach twisted now at the memory.

She watched Vanessa across the table, her own daughter slouched like a marionette with cut strings.

Vanessa had told her, years ago, that Bryson made her heart race. She had whispered it late one night, cheeks flushed, as if confessing a crime. Her mother had kissed her forehead, said nothing, and tucked her into bed.

She hadn't stopped the whispers when Delilah came around, when neighbors speculated, when Bryson's name became entwined with her daughter's like a knot in a seam. She hadn't stopped her own mother's mutterings about stitching blessings, securing futures. She hadn't cut the threads when she first noticed them.

And now her daughter sat here, silent and hollowed, because the plan had cracked around her.

Serena swallowed hard, forcing her voice calm. "Did you sleep at all?"

A humorless laugh escaped her daughter. "Does it matter?"

The words were sharp, brittle, like glass underfoot. They landed heavy in her chest. She wanted to reach across the table, cradle her daughter's hand, tell her she didn't need Bryson, didn't need perfection.

But the words stayed caged. Because saying them aloud would mean admitting her own part in all of it. That she had let the pattern repeat.

When Vanessa went upstairs, her shoulders still bent under invisible weight, Serena remained in the dining room. She sat in the quiet until the clock chimed noon, her coffee stone cold, her hands clenched around the china cup.

She thought of Irma. The woman was nearly a hundred. People called her gifted, touched. She called herself a helper of dreams. She stitched protection into Sunday coats, prosperity into work uniforms, fidelity into wedding gowns. Sometimes she stitched curses too, though no one used that word aloud. "Warding," she called it. "Securing."

But always, the stitches bound someone's life to someone else's will.

Delilah said she had known about Irma before they moved in across the way. She'd heard whispers of a seamstress who never used patterns, who saw things before they happened.

Over time, curiosity turned to need. Delilah told her she had ordered dresses for special occasions, table linens, even a christening blanket for a friend.

Her daughter's dress from the yacht still hung upstairs, and she knew, even without checking, that it carried Irma's hand.

She rose from the table, moving quietly up the stairs.

She didn't bother knocking. Her hand was already on the knob, her chest tight, her thoughts sharp.

The door swung open, and there was Vanessa in the dress from last night. It was draped around her like a spell that hadn't worn off. The lamp caught it in soft folds, making it shimmer, making it look dangerous.

Her daughter turned, startled. "Ma? What are you—"

She crossed the room in three quick strides. Her fingers found the hem, flipping it inside out, searching. Her hands trembled, but her eyes didn't waver. She knew what she was looking for. She could feel it before she saw it, the tight, unnatural knot stitched where no eye would look.

The scissors came out fast, gleaming under the light.

Snip.

"Ma!" Vanessa's voice pitched high, a mix of outrage and disbelief. She lurched back, nearly toppling her vanity stool. "Have you gone crazy? You're cutting my dress!"

Snip.

Her daughter's hand shot out, gripping her wrist. She could feel the heat of it, the fear beneath the anger.

"Stop!" Vanessa demanded. "What are you doing?"

But she pulled free and gathered the fallen threads quickly, curling them into her palm.

"No more," she whispered, her voice shaking. "No more."

Vanessa's eyes were wide, hurt, bewildered.

Her own reflection flashed in Vanessa's shocked eyes—wild, desperate, a mother who'd crossed a line and knew she'd do it again if she had to.

Her daughter would not live as she had lived. She would not be stitched into a life chosen by anyone else.

Serena would break the pattern, even if it broke her in the process.

♪ *At Last* — Etta James

23

Epilogue

Mayfield didn't need a folding chair.

She had brought her own. It was a low-backed rocker that creaked just enough to keep her company. She settled under the shade of the pecan tree in the far corner of the yard. From where she sat, she could see the whole afternoon stretch out before her like a quilt someone had taken their time piecing together.

The backyard was wide, new, clean. This house, this beautiful brick ranch, was the house Bryson and Marie had bought. A little big for just them, some might say, but Mayfield didn't. She understood what it meant for young folks to try and build something before life cracked them open. A home wasn't just walls. It was hope. And the food tastes better when the deed's in your name.

Smoke floated from the grill where the men gathered. Marie's father looked like he was telling a story, using the tongs like punctuation. Bryson's father laughed as women sat off to the side, fanning and watching.

Grace, her great-grand baby, was wiggling on her lap, all chubby knees and ponytails, warm and smelling like lotion and lemon. She clutched a plastic doll with a missing shoe in one hand, her other thumb stuck in her mouth. Every now and then she'd hum a tune only she seemed to know.

Her T-shirt read Buttah Baby, and Lord, if that wasn't the truth. The shirt wasn't store-bought either. Buttah Baby was the company Jaqueline and Marie ran together. Marie with her eye for beauty and order, Jaqueline with her sharp mind for money and marketing, pulling numbers and deals together like second nature. They'd moved the headquarters out west after Jaqueline married Tariq, but Sundays like this they always circled back.

Her eyes lingered on Marie and Jaqueline for a moment, both of them laughing as Grace squealed to be let down. She ran a few crooked steps before plopping down in the grass, barrettes bouncing, knees still a little dimpled with baby fat but long enough now to climb onto the porch by herself if no one stopped her.

"They selling care," Mayfield murmured, not to anyone in particular.

She gave a slow nod like that was something worth putting in the family Bible. "Women been doing that since the garden. They just gave it a name."

Mayfield didn't say much anymore. She rarely did unless it was necessary. She'd done her talking in her younger days, and she knew that watching sometimes told you more than words ever could.

She watched Marie move through the yard, barefoot, long dress swaying like praise music. She watched the way Bryson reached for her without thinking, like his hand was trained to find her. She watched Marie's mother smiling like a woman who had come through something and knew exactly how much it cost.

She looked at Jaqueline too, hair pulled back, her ring catching sunlight when she reached for her plate. That girl had always been a fighter, but now she carried it different, like she didn't have to prove it, only live it. Tariq sat beside her with his arm over her chair, gold in his smile.

Mayfield looked down at Grace again. Her thumb had slipped out of her mouth, lips parted as she whispered something to the doll, maybe a story, maybe a secret.

"She came from girls who knew how to survive," Mayfield thought. "Now she gets to learn how to rest."

The light filtered through the pecan leaves like honey, slow and generous.

A Southern girl's story never really ends, it just passes hands.

♪ *Simply Beautiful*- Al Green

Mayfield's Fried Catfish

A crispy, golden tradition that tastes like Sunday and stories on the porch.

Ingredients:

- 4 catfish fillets
- 2 cups buttermilk
- 1 cup cornmeal
- ½ cup all-purpose flour
- 1 tsp paprika
- 1 tsp garlic powder
- ½ tsp cayenne (optional)
- Salt and black pepper to taste
- Vegetable oil for frying

Instructions:

1. Rinse catfish and pat dry.
2. In a shallow dish, pour buttermilk over fillets. Let soak at least

30 minutes.

3. In another bowl, mix cornmeal, flour, paprika, garlic powder, cayenne, salt, and pepper.
4. Heat oil in a deep skillet over medium-high heat.
5. Remove fillets from buttermilk and coat evenly in cornmeal mixture.
6. Fry 3–4 minutes per side, or until golden brown and crisp.
7. Drain on paper towels.
8. Serve hot with hot sauce and love.

Mayfield's Tip: "The secret is in the soak."

Delilah's Peach Basil Mimosas

A polished twist on a Southern classic. Equal parts charm, intention, and sparkle.

Ingredients (makes 4):

- 1 bottle chilled Prosecco or Champagne
- 1 cup peach nectar or purée (Delilah prefers fresh, strained)
- 1 tbsp honey
- 1 tbsp fresh lemon juice
- 4–6 fresh basil leaves
- Thin peach slices for garnish

Instructions:

1. In a small pitcher, stir together peach nectar, honey, and lemon juice until blended.
2. Lightly press basil leaves between your palms to release aroma, then drop one into each flute.
3. Pour peach mixture into flutes, filling ⅓ of the way.

4. Slowly top with chilled Prosecco.
5. Garnish each glass with a thin peach slice or basil sprig.

Delilah's Tip: "Always use a chilled bottle, never stir after pouring, and serve in your best crystal. Presentation is half the experience."

Jaqueline's Sweet Tea Latte

A soul-soothing drink. Warm, creamy, and inspired by her shea butter business.

Ingredients:

- 2 black tea bags
- 1 cup hot water
- ½ cup warm milk (almond, oat, or whole)
- 1 tbsp honey or maple syrup
- ½ tsp vanilla extract
- Sprinkle of cinnamon

Instructions:

1. Steep tea bags in hot water for 3–5 minutes.
2. Stir in honey, vanilla, and cinnamon.
3. Warm milk until frothy and pour over tea.
4. Sip slow, preferably with a journal and soft playlist.

Jaqueline's Tip: "Good tea, like shea butter, reminds you to slow down and nourish yourself."

Renae's Backyard Pasta Salad

Bright, fresh, and full of flavor, just like Renae's laugh echoing through a summer cookout.

Ingredients:

- 1 box rotini pasta
- 1 cup cherry tomatoes, halved
- 1 cup cucumbers, diced
- ½ cup red onion, finely chopped
- 1 cup Italian dressing
- Salt and pepper to taste

Instructions:

1. Cook pasta according to package directions. Drain and rinse under cold water.
2. In a large bowl, combine pasta, tomatoes, cucumbers, and red onion.
3. Pour in Italian dressing and toss well.

4. Season with salt and pepper.
5. Chill at least 1 hour before serving.

Renae's Tip: "It tastes better the next day, if it lasts that long."

Marie's Chicken Fried Rice

Quick, comforting, and just the right mix of flavor and soul, Marie's go-to for busy nights.

Ingredients:

- 2 cups cooked rice (preferably day-old)
- 1 lb boneless chicken breast, diced
- 2 eggs, lightly beaten
- 1 cup frozen peas and carrots
- ½ onion, chopped
- 3 tbsp soy sauce
- 2 tbsp vegetable oil
- 1 tsp sesame oil
- Salt and pepper to taste
- Green onions for garnish

Instructions:

1. Heat 1 tbsp oil in a large skillet over medium heat. Cook chicken

until browned and done. Remove and set aside.

2. Add another tbsp oil. Sauté onions and vegetables until tender.
3. Push veggies to one side; pour eggs on the other. Scramble gently.
4. Add rice, cooked chicken, and soy sauce. Stir well to combine.
5. Drizzle sesame oil and season to taste.
6. Garnish with green onions and serve hot.

Marie's Tip: " I swear by using yesterday's rice. It soaks up the flavor."

Group Discussion Guide

1.Roots & Return: Marie begins the story back in her childhood home. How does returning home shape her choices, relationships, and the way she sees herself?

2.The Men in Their Worlds: The men in *Southern Girls* each play very different roles in the women's stories. How do they influence the women's growth, confidence, or struggles?

3.The World's Gaze: How does the world's view of pregnancy — especially for a young Black woman — shape Marie's choices and emotions? In what ways does she internalize society's judgment or expectation, and how does she ultimately reclaim her own narrative?

4.Love vs. Expectation: Several relationships in *Southern Girls* are tested by what's expected of them — family, faith, or social status. Which characters do you think chose love over expectation, and who didn't?

5.Mothers & Daughters: How do Renae and Marie's relationship patterns mirror or challenge one another? What does the story say about generational healing among women?

6.Secrets & Silence: Many of the characters keep things unsaid — from unspoken love to hidden pain. What are the consequences of those silences?

7.The Inner Girl: Throughout the story, traces of the girls each woman used to be lingers beneath who they've become. How do moments of vulnerability, fear, or joy reveal their younger selves? What does the story suggest about healing or honoring the girl we used to be?

8.Faith & Forgiveness: The story weaves faith through both comfort and conflict. How does spirituality influence the women's choices?

9.Legacy & Lineage: Family history plays a subtle but powerful role in the novel. What do you think the story is saying about what we inherit, and what we're allowed to change?

10.The Southern Girl in You: If you had to write your own chapter title beginning with *"The Girl Who..."* what would it be, and why?

Acknowledgments

To God — all glory and credit belong to You.

To my family, for holding me down through every "just one more chapter."

To my husband, my forever teammate, who never stops believing in me.

To my children, you are my reason and proof that love multiplies.

To my father and my all my "work moms," thank you for the prayers and for keeping me steady when I was juggling it all.

To my early readers — Chanterra, Amber, Janna, DeLanni, Brittany, and so many others — your early faith, encouragement, and feedback meant everything.

And to all the girls, young and grown, who will see pieces of themselves in these pages. Your strength, your softness, and your stories matter.

— Kat Ball

Want More?

There's a special bonus chapter waiting just for you!

Visit inkandhoneypress.com and join the email list to unlock your bonus chapter today! You'll also get early access to new releases, behind-the-scenes notes from the author, and other exclusive content!

About the Author

Kat Ball is an artist from Virginia whose writing celebrates love, legacy, and quiet strength. As wife and mother, she writes with the richness of home in her heart and the rhythm of life in her hands. Her debut novel, Southern Girls, is a love letter to faith, friendship, and the women who raise us.

www.ingramcontent.com/pod-product-compliance
Lightning Source LLC
Chambersburg PA
CBHW021414110726
47901CB00008B/2172